Just Plain Al

Just Plain Al

Constance C. Greene

A Yearling Book

Published by
Dell Publishing
a division of
The Bantam Doubleday Dell Publishing Group, Inc.
1 Dag Hammarskjold Plaza
New York, New York 10017

Yearling ® TM 913705, Dell Publishing, a division of the
Bantam Doubleday Dell Publishing Group, Inc.

ISBN: 0-440-40073-2

This edition published by arrangement with Viking Penguin Inc.

Printed in the United States of America

October 1988

10 9 8 7 6 5 4 3 2 1

CW

For Sophie and Samantha

Just Plain Al

chapter 1

"If I was pretty, with gorgeous long legs and big bosoms and tawny hair and all that junk," Al said, "Al might be OK. But with my equipment, Al stinks."

All morning we'd been trying to think of another nickname for Al. She's hitting the big one-four, fourteen, that is, next week, and she says she's too old to go on being called Al. It's a baby name, she says.

"I never knew a baby called Al," I told her. "Did you?"

"You know what I mean. I need something with pizzazz. I'm standing where the brook and the river meet, kid, and I want to tell you"—Al shot me a piercer—"it's a cold and lonely place."

"Yeah, and plenty wet, too," I said.

Oblivious to my sparkling wit, Al plunged on.

"How about Sandy? I think Sandy's kind of a cute name."

"Nope," I said firmly. "Sandy's out. People would only get you mixed up with Little Orphan Annie's dog."

"You're right." Al sighed. "Except he's much cuter'n me."

Oh, boy. Here we go again. Al was headed straight for the pits, a place she's quite familiar with.

"Besides," I said, "who has all that stuff, the legs, the bosoms, the hair, when they're fourteen? Nobody. Name me one person."

"Brooke Shields!" Al shouted. "Elizabeth Taylor! Plenty of people!"

"Brooke Shields hasn't got big bosoms," I said, remaining calm. Sometimes I act older'n Al, although she's a year older'n me. One of us has to remain calm in a crisis. Hardly a day passes without at least one.

"And furthermore," I said, "I read that Elizabeth Taylor has short, stubby legs."

"On her, who notices?" Al snapped, then got back to the matter at hand.

"I still think Alex has the most class." Al let her eyelids droop, which she always does when she imitates Greta Garbo. "Alex, Alex, my darling," she murmured in a deep voice. Then her eyes widened and she said, "Imagine anyone saying, 'Al, Al, my darling?' Absurd, *mes enfants*."

"I bet right at this moment Brian is practicing saying,

'Al, Al, my darling,' " I told her. Brian is a boy Al likes who lives near Al's father and stepmother in Ohio. He writes Al postcards. Well, actually, he's written her one postcard. It just seems like more.

"Don't be weird," Al said, but she perked up considerably at the mention of Brian's name.

"Stand over there," I directed. "And let me see if you could pass as an Alex."

Al did as she was told. She had on the red shoes she bought to wear to her father's wedding. She loves those shoes to death, even though they give her humongous blisters.

Al posed with one hand on her hip, knees bent in that asinine way models have. She pushed out her lips and dragged a strand of hair across her face so she'd look seductive and sexy. Like an Alex.

I circled her slowly, studying her, pretending I was a world-famous photographer lining her up for a glossy magazine spread.

"Snap it up. I haven't got all day," Al said.

"Tough. Neither do I." I narrowed my eyes at her. "Do you realize how much time we've spent trying to figure out a new name for you? Anyway, I think you're stuck with Al. It's you in a nutshell."

"That's what I'm afraid of." Al oozed out of her model's pose and looked dejected.

"I've got it!" Inspiration had struck me. "How about Zandra? If that isn't classy and loaded with pizzazz, I don't know what is."

"Zandra? What kind of a weirdo name is that?"

"I read about a dress designer called Zandra," I told Al. "She makes outrageously expensive clothes for the very rich. That's what it said. If the dress she's wearing is pink, she dyes her hair pink. If the dress is green, the hair is also green. I call that classy. And you've got to admit that Zandra would make you stand out in any crowd, *n'est-ce-pas?*"

"Zandra." Al tried it on for size, rolling the name around on her tongue to see if it fit. "Zandra, Zandra." Al grinned. "My mother would have a cow."

"You might get to like it," I said. I wasn't going to say anything, but at the moment, Al did not look like a Zandra. In addition to her red shoes, which have big clunky heels and make her walk sort of like Frankenstein, she had on a pair of ratty old jeans and her AL(exandra) the Great T-shirt. Her father and stepmother had sent it to her when Al's mother got pneumonia and had to go to the hospital. Al stuck by her mother instead of going to the barn dance in Ohio, which she so longed to do. Al wears that T-shirt almost every day. Sometimes she sleeps in it. If she was in a burning building and had to choose between it and her red shoes, Al says she'd take 'em both and Devil take the hindmost. Whatever *that* means.

"On second thought," I said, "maybe you're not a Zandra. That's a pretty fancy name."

"Yeah." Al flicked her eyelashes at me. "And I'm pretty plain. Just plain Al, they call me."

"I didn't mean that," I said.

"Listen," she told me.

"I'm listening."

"I read a book about shoes. It says that red shoes are a weapon. That red shoes make men perspire and stammer and pull at their neckties. Did you ever hear that?"

I shook my head.

"Well, if I ever get to the farm, I'll wear these beauties." Al stuck out a foot and we both stared at it. "And Brian will stammer and perspire and tug at his necktie, he'll be so crazy about me."

Al stopped talking. I knew she expected me to say something significant.

I thought a minute.

"You think Brian owns a necktie?" I said at last.

chapter 2

When I first knew Al, she had pigtails. She was the only girl in the whole entire school who had them. Al is a nonconformist and proud of it. She went to have her hair styled and came out with her pigtails intact. And it was her mother's hair stylist, working under orders from her mother.

Al's a year older than I am, due to the fact that she traveled around a lot when she was little and got left back somewhere along the line.

Al broods a lot. She spends too much time contemplating her own navel. Sometimes it gets me down. I love her. She's my best friend. I only wish she had a lighter heart. Last week she said to me, "Someday before I'm through with life, I would like to be three things. I would like to be thin, and delicate and radiant. That's not asking too much, do you think?"

I told her no, I didn't think it was asking too much. If I could be three things, I would like to be voluptuous and blithe and droll.

That night while I was washing the lettuce and Teddy was hurling knives and forks around in his version of setting the table, the doorbell rang.

"I'll get it!" Teddy hollered. I put out my foot and tripped him. He went sprawling. I let Al in. We stepped over Teddy, who was lying on the rug, sniveling. Al bent down to pat him on the head and he licked her hand, like a dog. She said, "Down, Fido," and Teddy doubled up, giggling.

"Hello, Al," my mother said. "How's your mother doing?"

"Fine, thanks. The doctor says she's almost good as new." Behind my mother's back Al waggled her fingers at me. She had something important to tell.

We zapped into my room and closed the door. I leaned against it, listening. Then I yanked it open, expecting Teddy to fall in. For once, he wasn't there. Teddy suffers from an advanced case of eavesdropitis.

What's up?"

Al's mouth curved upward. "Are you busy Saturday night?" she asked me in a happy voice.

"Sure. The opera, the Russian Tea Room, then on to Elaine's or perhaps Mortimer's." These are very "in" places in New York, where if you don't get a good table, you go home and shoot yourself. These are places were luminaries congregate. I've never been to a luminary place. Neither has Al. She goes to restaurants for dinner lots more than I do, though. Her mother's various beaux take her, in an attempt to buy her affections, she says. My mother doesn't have any beaux. She has only my father.

"How about going to the Rainbow Room for dinner?" Al said casually. The Rainbow Room is a fancy dancy place atop the RCA building in Rockefeller Center. The view is fantastic, I've heard. Needless to say, the Rainbow Room is very expensive.

"So long as it's your treat," I told her.

"Well, it just so happens my mother's new beau, Stan, is treating." Al smiled at me. Her teeth are very nice and she doesn't wear braces. I tell her to smile more often, but she says life is a serious business.

"I thought you were joking," I said. "Stan must have megabucks. How come he asked me? He doesn't even know me."

"If he did he might not've asked you," Al said, poking me to show she was only fooling. "He asked my mother to dine. She said she'd promised to take her daughter out to celebrate her birthday. And her daughter's little friend was coming, too."

"Is that me?"

"He said, 'Bring the little friend along, too. We'll make it a real party.' So how about it? Want to come?" Her eyes were very bright.

"I'll have to ask my mother. What happened to Mr. Wright?" Mr. Wright was Al's mother's beau before Stan showed up.

"Oh, he was so cheerful all the time she was in the hospital, she said he depressed her, so she told him to take a walk," Al said.

"I don't have anything to wear to the Rainbow Room," I said. "What are you wearing?"

"Lord knows." Al's eyebrows disappeared underneath her bangs. "My mother might buy me a black satin strapless number if she can find one on sale. I plan to wear my red shoes with it and maybe get some red lace stockings to add the final touch. Really make those bozos at the Rainbow Room sit up and take notice, huh?" Al did a little belly dance and a few bumps and grinds to show me she was still in shape.

Teddy's voice came through the keyhole, announcing, "Dinner is served, folks." Al flung open the door and almost knocked out Teddy's teeth. "*Scusa, scusa,*" Al said, planting a big juicy kiss on Teddy's cheek, thereby stopping him from hollering and claiming damages. Then she disappeared with the speed of light, and we sat down to dinner.

"Dad," I said, "did red shoes ever make you stammer and pull at your necktie in confusion?"

"No, I can't say they ever did," my father said. "But I

once had a pair of brown shoes that did exactly that. They were too tight. How did you know?"

"I meant red shoes on a lady," I said.

"In my day no lady would be caught dead wearing red shoes," my father said.

"*Quel* bummer. I heard red shoes were a secret weapon and make men go cuckoo pots over a girl who wears them."

"My friend Hubie has red sneakers," Teddy put in his oar, "and nobody goes cuckoo pots over him."

"Al asked me to go to the Rainbow Room Saturday night," I said, ignoring Teddy. "Her mother's new beau is taking us to celebrate Al's birthday." My mother and father raised their eyebrows in unison. They've been married so long they tend to react to startling news in identical fashion.

"The only trouble is," I said, playing it cool, "I don't have anything to wear."

Teddy lined up peas on his knife.

"Your Easter dress will be perfect," my mother said.

"You mean the blue one?" I said, choking just a little.

"I love that dress on you." My mother smiled at me. Teddy dipped his head, keeping a close eye on the peas.

"That's enough." My mother spoke from the corner of her mouth, which she does very well. Teddy let the peas slide off, pretending he hadn't known they were there.

I'm talking Rainbow Room here, Ma, I thought, not Easter bunnies.

"It doesn't fit," I said.

"What's a beau?" Teddy asked.

"A male friend," my mother answered.

"Hubie must be my beau, then." Teddy knows just how to touch a nerve.

"Hubie is your friend," my mother said firmly.

"It's too small," I said.

"Is that the one that makes your rear end wiggle?" Teddy looked up at me with guileless eyes.

My father tuned in at last, the way he does.

"Well, I guess we don't want our little darling going to the fleshpots in a dress that makes her rear end wiggle," he said. "I guess we can spring for a new dress for such an august occasion." Then my father excused himself. He had work to do.

The telephone rang. It was my mother's sister, reporting on her ex-husband's doings. Teddy and I sat at the table, alone.

A rush of love for my dear little brother flooded me.

"I might just kiss you, Ted," I told him.

A look of sheer amazement and terror crept over his greasy little face. His knife shot out, a dagger held at the ready. Keeping me at bay.

"I thought August was a month," Teddy said.

chapter 3

The next morning, when Al answered her door, I said in a snooty voice, "Podden me, but is Zandra at home, perchance?"

Al made a megaphone with her hands and hollered, "Hey, Zandra, some weird dude's out here looking for you!" then, flashing a phony smile, she held out a limp hand and said, "Oh, hi! I had a simply super time last night! My date was super! The party was super! He asked me to go to the junior prom. He's also a super dancer!"

"Super!" I said, and we collapsed on each other and laughed for about five minutes.

"Is your mother up yet?" I asked. Al's mother wears

sleep shades to shut out the light. She has about a thousand little pillows on her bed. When she wants to go to sleep, she tosses all the little pillows on her *chaise longue*. That's French for daybed. The *chaise longue* is strictly to lie on during the day. I think you're also supposed to eat bonbons and read dirty French novels on it, too. Life gets very complex when one gets older and has French furniture, it seems.

"She's gone to work already." Al made a face. She's always trying to mother her mother. This is role reversal, Al says, and is due to the fact that her mother is divorced and has been sick and needs someone to lean on.

I followed her into the apartment. I could smell coffee. I like the smell but I hate the taste of coffee.

"What's the word?" Al asked.

"If the invite's still good, my parents said I could have new duds for the Rainbow Room," I said. I hope Al's mother and her new beau don't break up before I get a chance to check out the Rainbow Room. You never know.

"Excellent, excellent!" Al did a couple of expert bumps and grinds. She could be a burlesque queen if only burlesque wasn't dead. She also does a pretty fair belly dance. We were going to take lessons in belly dancing, but we never got around to it.

Al and her mother moved down the hall from us last fall. This is the first birthday we've celebrated together. Mine is next month, so that'll be the second.

"My mother says shopping with me drains her emotionally," I told Al, "so that leaves you."

"I will be your duenna, child," she said. "Just wait'll I empty the garbage."

We fought our way through the mirrors on Bloomingdale's ground floor. The salesgirl in the junior dress department gave us a disenchanted look. Probably her feet hurt already, and she figured us for a couple of deadbeats. And rightly so.

"Have you anything on sale?" Al asked. She was her mother's own child. Al's mother always buys her stuff on sale. "She'll grow into it," Al's mother says.

"Not at this time of year." The salesgirl sniffed. "Can I help you with anything?"

"Actually, we're looking for something that would be appropriate for dining at the Rainbow Room," Al said, sniffing back.

The girl looked us over.

"What size?" Her gaze skimmed the tops of our heads.

"Petite," Al said.

"Ah, yes, petite." The girl smiled. "Perhaps something on this rack might do. Call me if you see something you like."

We went through the rack in record time. "My mother says they never tell their right size," Al said. "If they're above a size twelve, they lie. If you ask me, people in this country think too much about what size they are. Take Russia. I bet they don't think about sizes in Russia."

We didn't find anything at Bloomie's, so we decided to go across to Alexander's, where it's much cheaper. On our way out we stopped at the food shop. Bloomie's is famous for its exotic goodies. They frequently hand out free samples. Last time we got a memorable chocolate-chip cookie.

A girl wearing a peasant costume handed us a little square of something attached to a toothpick. We each took one.

"What is it?" Al asked, putting hers in her mouth. She must've been very hungry. Usually Al wants to know what she's eating.

"Headcheese," the girl said, flashing her gums at us.

"What's it made of?"

"Actually, it's got a bit of this and a bit of that in it." I think she was Danish.

"Are you Danish?" I asked her.

"On my mother's side." She had very long gums.

"What's 'a bit of this and a bit of that' mean?" Al stopped chewing. Her cheek bulged where she'd stored her free sample.

"A bit of the tongue, a bit of the brains, too. As well as the head, of course. Hence the name 'headcheese.' " The girl's eyes were very bright as she studied Al's face. Al has one of those faces that shows everything.

"Whose head?" Al managed to get out.

"The calf, or maybe the pig's. It depends."

Slowly, slowly, Al spit out what was left of her free sample. Mine lay heavy at the bottom of my stomach.

"Is there a trash can around?" Al whispered, not looking at what lay in her palm.

"Gee, I don't know," the girl said brightly. "I'm only here for the day."

Al stomped off. I had a hard time keeping up. She went through the revolving door like a whirling dervish and hit the street at a gallop.

"Did you hear her? I almost barfed!" Al clutched her throat. "I almost lost my cookies all over Bloomie's food shop. Do you think she was putting us on? Do you think she made that up?"

"No," I said, "I think she was telling the truth."

"I have a feeling this is not my day," Al said. Somehow we'd lost our interest in shopping. "Look," I said, pointing. "There's one of those cheapo hot dog wagons on the corner. Let's get one." Despite the headcheese inside me, I was hungry.

"You're kidding me!" Al yelled, still clutching her throat. "I may never eat again. Besides, you know what they say is in hot dogs. Unspeakable ingredients. Dog's hair, sweepings off the floor, and worse."

"With sauerkraut," I said. "And lots of mustard!"

"Oh, well." Al was a pushover for hot dogs. "With all that stuff on it, we won't even be able to tell it's a hot dog, right?"

It was one of those days that sometimes drops down at the end of summer. Just when you think fall will never come, there it is, like a present. As we headed for the hot dog wagon, I saw the man. He was one of those New York crazies. Shouting, gesticulating, he lurched through the crowd. People tucked in their elbows to make a path for him, pretending he wasn't really there. He was harmless. No one so much as flicked an eye in his direction.

"Let's cross," I whispered. I'm chicken. I'm always afraid guys like him might say or do something. I don't know what I'd do if he did.

Al had her hot dog money out, held high in her hand. It was then that I saw the woman. She was standing on the corner under the digital clock over the bank. It was 1:24. The temperature was 72 degrees. The woman's face was so deeply red it was almost purple. She wore a filthy gray sweater and billowy pants held up by rope. Her hands were huge and swollen, the same color as her face. She held a sign that read Please Help Me.

Al saw the woman the same instant I did. She veered toward her without missing a beat, the dollar bill waving in the wind. I knew Al was going to give the woman her money.

The man swooped without warning. He snatched the money out of Al's hand and took off, darting and dodging into the crowd. The Artful Dodger had nothing on him.

"Hey!" Al bellowed. "Catch him! Police!" Several people turned to stare, but nobody got excited. Things like that happen every day. I stayed where I was and watched Al also disappear into the crowd in pursuit.

I wanted to leave, wanted to forget the sight of the woman standing there holding her sign, but I didn't dare. In a strange way, I felt responsible for her. She had turned to stone and stood, eyes closed, as if she couldn't bear another thing.

If Al caught up with the man, what would happen? Maybe he'd turn on her, attack her. I should've gone with her. My feet wouldn't move. I felt as if I'd been glued to the sidewalk.

I shivered, the way you do when someone walks over your grave. Then, just when I was giving up, I saw Al threading her way through the throng of shoppers. Her face was scarlet, and perspiration ran down the sides of her face.

"Can you believe that creep?" A mustache of sweat glistened on her upper lip. "That lousy creep took it right out of my hand."

The woman opened her eyes and looked straight at us. They tell you to avoid eye contact. Yet we looked into her eyes. They were dark gray or maybe blue. I couldn't be sure. I fumbled in my pocket and came up with eighty cents, all I had. I held the money out to her. She wouldn't look down at my hand, only in my eyes.

Then I saw her hand creep out, cupped into a little bowl, its broken fingernails curved jaggedly over the tips of her fingers. I put the eighty cents into the little bowl. Her eyes never wavered. I was the first to look away. Maybe she was deaf and dumb, I thought. Maybe that was it. Then she said something to me, maybe thanks, maybe not. Maybe she was cursing me. I couldn't tell.

"What's going on here, anyway?" Al said. "How come all these people are starving? How come all these fat cats are eating caviar and lots of people don't even have a place to sleep when it gets cold? I don't get it. How come things are so uneven?"

Al shook her head despairingly. Her face was bleak.

"What can she buy with eighty cents?" I asked. Al didn't answer me. We walked all the way home, thirty blocks, without talking to each other.

There was nothing to say.

chapter 4

All that night, awake or asleep, I kept seeing the woman's face. She and her children probably lived in one horrible little room filled with cockroaches, which scuttled under the bed and kept them awake all night. And the hallways were filled with strange, lurking people, with gray faces, making odd noises. And the children cried a lot because their stomachs were empty. It must be terrible to be really hungry. And to have no money to buy food. Sometimes, when I'm hungry after school, I try to imagine how I'd feel if there were no food in the house and no prospect of any. I can't imagine what it's really like, but I try.

So I gave her eighty cents. Big deal. I was ashamed of giving her so little, even though it was all I had.

In the morning I leaned against the sink and drank my orange juice and watched my mother getting ready to go out. This was her day to work at the hospital thrift shop. They were pricing donations today, she told me, to prepare for the grand opening next week.

"If I see a dress that might suit you," she told me, "I'll bring it home with me. We get some very nice things there."

"A secondhand dress for the Rainbow Room?" I tried not to sound snotty. And failed. My mother is a scrounge. She can always find a way to beat the high cost of living. My father says she works miracles, but I wish she wouldn't try to work one on me.

My mother shot me a dark look. "There are plenty of people who would be glad to be given some secondhand things," she reminded me. "There are also people who never wear anything but other people's castoffs. Don't be a snob."

After my mother had given me a cool cheek-brush in farewell and told me to put some potatoes on to boil for potato salad, I was alone. Teddy had gone to day camp. So there I was, sitting in the kitchen, alone with the clicking refrigerator, the dripping faucet, and myself. Being by yourself isn't always easy, especially if yourself turns out to be a not-so-nice person.

I've gotten much more introspective since I've known Al. Before she came into my life, I was a happy-go-lucky slob. Now I tend to brood, though not nearly as much as she does. Al says knowing me has made her much more laid back than she used to be. I guess we're good for each other, the way friends should be.

When you come right down to it, though, I'll be thirteen in September and what have I got to show for it?

Nada, as Al would say.

Then Polly called. Boy, was I glad to hear her cheerful little voice!

"You sound like you've lost your last friend," Polly told me. "And you haven't. Here I am."

She asked me and Al over for supper. "I'm making chicken cacciatore tonight," Polly said. "The *spécialité de la maison.*" Polly is a star cook. She's going to be a chef and have her own restaurant when she's eighteen.

"Sounds good," I said. Polly and Al and I are all very different. Polly stayed at our apartment when her parents went to Africa, and Al got a little uptight. Two's company, three's a crowd, as my mother says in her infinite wisdom. And she's right. Al flailed around awhile, then she got over whatever was bugging her, and now we all get along fine. We laugh a lot. Mr. Richards said a good laugh was good for the soul. He also was right.

Mr. Richards died eight months ago. He was the assistant super in our building. He was also our friend. Not a day goes by but that something he said or did doesn't remind us of him.

"You go," Al said when I told her Polly had invited us. "I'm always horning in. Polly's your friend, after all."

"Don't be a klutz," I told her. "She's your friend, too. Polly doesn't ask anyone she doesn't like. You know that."

Al smiled. "Yeah, I guess you're right."

"Polly's making chicken cacciatore."

"Is that anything like headcheese?" Al asked nervously.

The dictionary said "cacciatore" means cooked with tomatoes and various herbs.

"Whew! That was close." Al wiped off imaginary perspiration on her sleeve. "I better leave my mother a note. She's dining with Stan again tonight." Al rolled her eyes. "I think it's serious."

"I've heard that one before," I said. "Remember when you thought she was going to marry Ole Henry and go to Bermuda on her honeymoon?"

"Yeah, well, I called that one wrong, all right," Al admitted. "But there's something about the way her voice goes all soft and cuddly when she says 'Stan' that makes me think this might be the real thing."

Al's mother is loaded with sex appeal. For a woman her age, I mean. She must be at least forty. Maybe more. But I've noticed that whenever one of her beaux takes a walk, there's another one standing in line. I wonder if my mother has sex appeal. If she and my father ever get divorced, would men line up to take *her* out? Well, they might take her, and even me, but one thing is sure: we'd have to drown Teddy.

"Listen," I said, "if her face goes all soft and cuddly over a name like Stan, it must be love."

"I didn't say 'face,' dummy, I said voice. Do you realize if she gets married to Stan, I'd probably move away, probably to a mansion in the suburbs, and we wouldn't be best friends, anymore? You and Polly would be best friends."

Before my very eyes, Al's face grew long and doleful. "Of course," she said, "I'd invite you to sleep over, meet my new friends, stuff like that, but it definitely wouldn't be the same. As living down the hall, I mean."

Holy Toledo. Al's mother hardly knows this Stan guy and already they're moving to a mansion in the suburbs.

"What's eating you? One minute everything's fine, and the next you're all bent out of shape."

"Sorry," Al said. "I'm uptight. Yesterday freaked me out."

"You're probably going through the change of life," I told her. "Thirteen is one thing, fourteen is another. Fourteen is practically sixteen, and we all know what that means. You're a woman when you hit sixteen."

"Yeah," Al agreed, "that's it. My hormones are bent out of shape, too. You called it."

"Your mansion, the one you're moving to, does it have a Jacuzzi?" I wanted to kid Al, make her laugh.

"You got it, baby." Al grinned at me. "And a hot tub. Hot tubs are very big in the 'burbs, I hear."

"Did you tell your mother? About yesterday?" I asked her.

"Nope. Did you?" I shook my head. We don't tell our mothers lots of things. We protect them from the facts of life.

"Just give them what they want," my mother is always telling me. "Just hand it over and they'll leave you alone." My mother is sometimes quite naive. But I don't have any gold chains, or an expensive wristwatch, or any cash. I figure I'm pretty safe. I know enough not to walk down alleys or in bad neighborhoods. I know not to cut through Central Park, ever. Or to open the door to a guy dressed in a Santa Claus suit who says he's selling Girl Scout cookies.

Al and I have a lot of street smarts.

But you know mothers.

chapter 5

The elevator had barely come to a stop before Polly flew out and hugged us both. For a skinny person loaded with bones, Polly is surprisingly strong. "Boy, am I glad to see you!" she cried. "I thought you'd never get here. Come on in."

Polly's apartment smelled delicious, as always. We followed her into the kitchen and sat on high stools watching her grate and mince and chop. Polly could be on television, she really could. She can talk and cook at the same time. And that's not easy. I tried it and I know. I almost took my thumb off.

"We have the joint to ourselves," Polly said. Her parents were at a diplomatic reception, and Evelyn, Polly's sister, was in the Maine woods. "She's doing research." Polly sighed. "She's in love with this handsome forest ranger, and she figures she better learn how to chop wood and build fires without matches, all that junk. She doesn't even have a telephone up there. My father says that means she's serious about the guy. My mother said she better watch out for bears. The Maine woods are loaded with bears, and they eat people if provoked. My father says forget the bears, he's saving money hand over fist with Evelyn out of reach of a telephone."

We watched, silent with awe, as Polly diced a defenseless tomato.

"How's Thelma?" Al asked when Polly had finished dicing.

"Thelma's in a dither," Polly said, throwing onions and peppers into a big pot. Thelma's this really shallow person who's friends with Polly. Al and I can't figure out how a good, true-blue person like Polly can be friends with a shallow person like Thelma.

"What's she dithering about?" I said.

"Well, her parents told her she can have either a new car or a nose job when she turns sixteen," Polly said.

Al and I looked at each other.

"Which did she choose?" Al wanted to know.

Polly finished browning some chicken legs, then turned down the heat and put a lid on the pot.

"A nose job."

I laughed. For some reason this struck me as very funny. Al's face was inscrutable.

"What kind of a car did they have in mind?" Al finally said.

Polly shrugged. "Who knows? Maybe a Chevvy. Nothing fancy."

"I never even noticed Thelma's nose," I said.

"It's not really gross. She can live with it, she says. She's been living with it for almost thirteen years, right?" Polly said. "Thelma broke it when she was four, going the wrong way down a one-way street. She totaled her tricycle. They set it wrong, I guess. Anyway, it's got this big bump. Thelma's very self-conscious about her nose.

"Besides," Polly threw a pinch of salt into the pot, "Thelma wants to be a rock star. She figures a cute nose is very important to a rock star."

Al started choking, she was laughing so hard. I thumped her on the back. "Cool it," I told her in a low voice. Thelma was Polly's friend, after all.

"Thelma a rock star?" Al said, sort of gurgling. "How come? She has a terrible voice."

"So what's that got to do with being a rock star?" Polly said. "She plans on dying her hair bright red and wearing really outrageous clothes and makeup. Then she'll go to a special school where they'll teach her all the moves, what you do with your hands, all that stuff. Then you memorize some lyrics and practice like mad in front of the mirror, and if you get a good agent, he gets you a couple of spots and you get some publicity, like your picture in magazines and all, and you're on your way.

"Of course, all this is three years away, so it gives Thelma time to get her act together. She thinks her life is going to change when she gets her new nose. I told her to take it slow, but you know Thelma."

"Yeah," Al said in a slow, wicked drawl.

"Thelma's father says he'll spring for part but not all of the expense. A good plastic surgeon costs big bucks." Polly went on. "So Thelma's saving her allowance like mad. We went shopping the other day, and everything she fell in love with she didn't buy. She tried on a sensational pair of pants but didn't buy them; she'd tried on some shoes, she didn't buy 'em; she even tried on a fake fur coat."

"Yeah, I bet she didn't buy it, either, right?"

"Hey, it's Thelma's nose, not mine," Polly said. "Give me a break."

For some reason both Al and I started to tell Polly about the man who'd snatched Al's money and the woman with the sign saying Please Help Me.

"I chased him," Al said, "but he got away."

"She wouldn't let me look away," I told Polly. "I thought she might be deaf and dumb, then she said something to me, only I couldn't understand her."

"Oh, boy," Polly said. "That sounds like something that might happen in Africa." With a long-handled fork, she poked at the chicken and said it was done.

We sat down and dug in. After a couple minutes of silence broken only by sounds of chewing, Al said, "This is the best."

"Uh-*huh*," I said. "Tell Polly about the headcheese," I told Al.

Al really knows how to tell a story. By the time she was

halfway through, we were all practically rolling on the floor.

"So I wanted to spit it out, but there wasn't a waste-basket around, and I held it in my hand until we got outside. That's the last time I'm eating any old free sample," Al said.

"Next time you come I'm fixing a headcheese soufflé," Polly said, wiping her eyes. "How's your mother doing, Al?"

The smile dropped off Al's face and bounced on the floor.

"She's fine, thanks, Polly," Al said, dead serious, "but my name's not Al any more."

"It's not? What is it, then?" Nothing surprises Polly.

"I can't decide. Maybe Sandy. Or Alex. Or how about Zandra?"

Polly said, "Why not stick with Al?"

"I can't exactly explain," Al said, frowning down at her plate, "but I'm hitting fourteen next week, and I figure it's time to have a more dignified name. One with more"—she looked over at me—"more pizzazz."

I decided to stay out of it. I'd heard it before. This was Polly's first time.

"Well, you're definitely not a Sandy," Polly said, frowning. "And I know a very snotty girl named Alex, so that's out. And as for Zandra—" Polly turned her thumbs down. "That's for a phony, and I know you, Al, you're no phony," Polly said.

"What else is there? I can't pick something entirely different. I have to stay in the Al range."

"Al is you in a nutshell," Polly said. "True blue, down to earth, no fooling around. You look like an Al."

I could tell from Al's face that Polly had unwittingly struck again. When Al was agitating about mailing her famous letter to Brian, like when should she mail it, what day would it arrive, etc., Polly got impatient and said, "Just mail the dumb thing," or something like that. I'll never forget Al's face when Polly said that. For a basically tactful person, Polly can be blunt at times.

"I told you!" Al wailed. "Just plain Al. That's me. When I'm an old lady in my rocking chair, I'll still be just plain Al. That's very depressing, you know that? How'd you like to be just plain anything?"

I could see her point. And I could see Polly knew she'd blown it.

"Listen, with three great minds at work," Polly tried to soothe Al, "I'm sure we'll come up with something. What's your middle name, Al?"

"I'm not telling," Al said.

"She's just trying to help," I said.

Al mumbled something. "Speak up," I said. Finally Al said, "Agnes," in a loud voice. Then louder. "Agnes!" she shouted. "It's Agnes! Put that in your pipe and smoke it!"

Both Polly and I knew when to quit. Polly brought out her chocolate brownie pudding for dessert.

"Calorie city," Al said, smacking her lips. On the way home she said, "I must've put on five pounds tonight."

"It's only baby fat," I told her.

"When you hit fourteen, it's gross, grown-up fat, kid,"

Al said. "What do you know? You're skinny. You don't know squat about being fat. People who've never been fat should keep their mouths shut. If you ask me, that is."

I opened my mouth to say I hadn't asked her, then closed it. I was beginning to wish Al would stay thirteen. For a while, anyway. This change of life stuff was getting rough. It looked to me as if the brook and the river were rising to flood stage and Al had better practice her backstroke, as well as her crawl.

chapter 6

My mother brought me home a dress from the thrift shop in a brown paper bag. Like a salami sandwich. It cost five bucks. I didn't want to like it, but even before I tried it on, I did. Then when I actually put it on and turned in front of my mother's full-length mirror, I tried not to smile. It was perfect. Oh, my basic stick figure was there, all right, lurking under the folds of striped taffeta, but still, I looked pretty neat. The dress did things for me.

My mother sat back on her heels, surveying the pinned-up hem.

"I must say I outdid myself," she said smugly.

"It's still too long," I said.

"Absolutely perfect. You're all set."

"How about shoes? And panty hose?"

"Shoes? Panty hose?" my mother repeated as if I'd spoken in Arabic.

"Well," I told her, "my dress was practically free, after all, and you don't expect me to go to the Rainbow Room in sneakers, do you? And I can't very well go barefoot, either. So what do you suggest?"

"Don't get snippy," my mother warned me.

Al rang her special ring. I let her in. "How do you like it?" I whirled for her benefit. "It's the bargain of the century. My mother is very pleased with herself for finding it. Come on into her room. She's shortening it."

If I hadn't been so entranced with myself, I would've noticed Al's grim expression. She stomped along behind me as I led her to my mother's *boudoir*. That's French for bedroom.

"Hello, Al," my mother greeted her.

Al said hello back. She didn't go into her routine about not being called Al any more. She simply plopped into my mother's boudoir chair, another thrift-shop bargain. The chair's bottom gave way, and Al's bottom hit the floor with an enormous thud.

"Oh, my gosh!" she cried, struggling to escape the chair's clutching arms. "I'm sorry! I'll pay to get it fixed. I'm so sorry!"

"It's not your fault, Al," said my mother, stretching out a hand to help her up. "It's needed fixing for some time. Don't worry about it."

"Boy, that's a relief. I thought I'd totaled it. I'm such a klutz."

"No, you're not," my mother said. To me she said, "Please take off your dress, and watch the pins. I'll get to it tonight."

After my mother made off with my dress over her arm, I stood in my underwear and watched Al pace.

"What's eating you?" I asked. In a minute she'd have to go to the bathroom.

"How'd you like my dress? My mother got it at the thrift shop. For five bucks. It's really spiffy, don't you think? I didn't want to let on how much I liked it or she'll never buy me anything in a department store ever again," I said laughing.

"I have to go to the bathroom," Al said. "Excuse me."

When she came back I told her I was getting heels and panty hose tomorrow. "What are you going to wear?" I said. "Did your mother bring you home anything yet?"

"What for?" Al went over to the window and stared out.

"For Saturday night is what for," I reminded her. "For your birthday dinner."

Al turned and looked at me.

"It's off," she said glumly.

"What do you mean? What's off?" I knew in my heart what she meant, but I had to hear her say it.

"No Rainbow Room. No celebration. *Nada.* I'll be lucky to get a burger at Burger King."

I couldn't speak. I was stunned.

"Stan, the one who was taking us there," Al said, "well, he had to go to Europe for a couple of weeks. He told my mother we'll do it when he gets back. I say forget the whole thing. My mother says she'll take us, but I told her no. It's too expensive. It's not worth it. It's too much money. And for what?" Al whirled on me and I backed off, arms crossed on my chest, suddenly cold.

"For a single lousy dinner, that's what. With all the people starving in the world, who needs it?"

"That's OK," I said, trying to hide my disappointment, "we'll think of something to do to celebrate."

Al trudged to the door as if her red shoes weighed a ton. "Hope you're not too disappointed."

"Hey, it's your birthday, not mine," I said.

"I'm sorry I made such a big deal out of it."

"It's OK," I said again. "Is your mother mad?"

"Mad at who?"

"Stan."

"He can't always call the shots. He's always hopping on a plane to go somewhere. He's an international banker."

"That's why he makes megabucks," I said.

"Yeah, I guess. Anyway, I'll just curl up with a good book. Beats indigestion, huh?" Al's eyes reminded me of a picture I'd seen of a baby deer caught in a trap: huge, liquid, sad. She did a couple of halfhearted bumps and grinds, but without her usual flair.

"I eat too much, anyway," she said. "Have a weird day."

"You, too," I told her.

After she'd gone, I stayed put, telling myself not to be a baby. It was her birthday, not mine, as I'd said. Good thing my mother bought the dress for a measly five bucks. Good thing she hadn't sprung for fifty.

I don't know who felt worse, Al or me.

I'll probably never know.

chapter 7

"Maybe they're mad at me," Al said. We were walking downtown to save bus fare. We planned on giving the money we'd saved to the needy. It was Al's idea.

"I bet they won't remember my birthday." Al was talking about her father and Louise and why she hadn't heard from them.

"It's not your birthday yet, don't forget," I told her. "How come you're making a Federal case out of turning fourteen? I think it'd be a neat age to be. You get to do all kinds of things you can't do when you're thirteen."

"What?"

"I can't think of anything right now. My mother says

thirty's the worst birthday. She said when she hit thirty, she felt ready for the old folks' home."

We waited for the red light to change.

"Maybe Brian will send you a birthday card," I said.

Al let out a mammoth Bronx cheer, scattering some pigeons freeloading on the sidewalk. My grandfather is the only person I know who can do a better Bronx cheer than Al. He says they used to call it a raspberry. It's something you do with your lips and tongue that makes a loud, rude noise. I'm not very good at it. I practice sometimes when I'm alone but don't seem to get much better.

"He won't even know it *is* my birthday," Al said. "How will he know? Unless, of course, he runs into Louise at the store and she says, 'Oh, Brian'—Al imitated Louise's voice—'Sunday is Al's birthday.' Then Brian says, 'Al, Al, who's she? Oh, yeah, the fat one with the glasses.' "

"Who says your self-confidence level is low?" I asked her sarcastically. "Whoever says that is a total nerd." Al is always taking tests in magazines to determine her level of self-confidence. Usually she ends up with a rating of "low," or sometimes, if she cheats a little, she gets a "medium." I crossed my eyes at her and she burst out laughing. Good. I had made her laugh at herself, no small feat.

"Hey, cool!" Al spied two slinky leather dresses with sequins on them, one black, one red, in a shopwindow. We blew on the glass and wrote our initials in the fog.

"Too bad we're not going to the Rainbow Room. That would be perfect."

"Yeah, you could buy the red and I'd buy the black," I said.

"Or better yet," Al said, "we can come back here tonight and break the glass and just reach in and take 'em."

Two women who were standing beside us making clucking sounds of dispproval at the leather dresses turned to stare at us. When they heard what Al said about breaking in, the women clutched their shoulder bags, looked alarmed, and backed away from us.

Refreshed by this encounter, we sauntered along Fifth Avenue, hoping we'd run into Rudy. He plays the violin on corners along Fifth Avenue. He is a first-rate violin player. Sometimes he migrates over to Broadway. Broadway's his favorite, he says, but the tips are better on Fifth. Rudy can play just about anything. "Just name me a tune and it's yours," he likes to say.

Sure enough. We were crossing Fifty-seventh Street when we heard violin music. We caught sight of Rudy through the crowd. He wore his houndstooth jacket with matching hat, which, he told us, his mother had made for him. And even though it was hot that day, he looked fine. He had a bunch of his political campaign buttons pinned to his jacket. Rudy collects them. He told us he's apolitical, which means he doesn't take sides. He just likes the buttons.

Today he had on the one that said I Like Ike, as well

as Down with McKinley, and his favorite, the one that says President Thomas E. Dewey.

When he saw us, he started to play "Thank Heaven for Little Girls." He always plays that one for us. Sometimes, if he's feeling frisky, he sings along with the music, imitating Maurice Chevalier. Rudy speaks seven languages, all in broken English, he says. Rudy is a native of Brooklyn. He was born on a roller coaster at Coney Island, he told us. His mother couldn't get off in time.

A bunch of camera-carrying Japanese businessmen stopped to listen. Rudy segued into "Japanese Sandman." He boasts there's not a person he can't match the song to. When he'd finished, the men clapped and asked if they could take his picture. Some put money into the open violin case Rudy kept at his feet. Rudy tipped his hat and said, *"Sayonara."* When they'd gone Rudy picked up the money and put it in his pocket.

"First folding money today," he told us. "Things are slow. At this rate, I'll be on the dole by week's end. Maybe I'll have to go back to my wife." He winked at us. Rudy lives alone in a hotel off Broadway. He likes it over there, he says, close to the theater district. The air's more exciting, more pulsating, he says. He eats all his meals in a deli around the corner from his hotel. For breakfast he eats a pastrami sandwich on rye, with pickles and relish.

"A little Mozart for you," he told us and broke into a Mozart concerto. Mozart's his favorite. "You'd be surprised the people who stop to listen to the old boy. The Master. They don't tip the way folks do for the golden

43

oldies, that's true, but there's lots of real music lovers out there. Warms my heart if not my palm."

Rudy is always joking with us. "You girls win the lottery yet?" he asked us. "Thought I saw you on TV the other night, picking up your prize. No? Wasn't you? Too bad. I was gonna ask could I borrow a couple hundred simoleons from you. A story for you: a lady leaves a mink coat in my friend's cab. He sees it laying there, returns it to the hotel he left the lady at, thinks he hears noises coming from it. He goes inside, the lady's having hysterics. 'My baby, my baby,' she's crying. My friend hands over the mink. The lady busses my friend, a big hug, big kiss, no money for his honesty, though. Then she reaches in and hauls out one of them little foreign dogs with a face on it only a mother could love. She goes kissy, kissy to the mutt, and that's that. No tip, no nothing. Next time my friend says he keeps the coat and leaves the country. How's that for a story?"

"I never know whether to believe you or not," Al said.

"You better believe me, sweetheart," Rudy said. "I was stolen by gypsies from my ancestral castle. The moat wasn't working that day, which is how the gypsies wormed their way in. So then they try to sell me back to my mother, the queen. She says, 'Has he got a little birthmark the shape of a star on his knee?' The gypsies say, 'Sure, he's got one just like that.' So my mother, the queen, screams, 'He ain't mine, then. My baby didn't have a mark on him!' "

Rudy broke into "Way down upon the Swanee River,"

accompanied by a soft-shoe routine. Quite a few people stopped to watch, clapping along, smiling. It was Rudy's kind of crowd. He was once a vaudeville star, he told us. The roar of the greasepaint, the smell of the crowd, was what counted, he said.

We waved and walked on.

"The one about the lady with the mink coat might've been true," I said, "but the gypsy story was a phony. That I know."

Al rolled her eyes at me. We stopped for another look at the leather dresses. They were gone from the window. The mannequins stared out at us, naked as jaybirds. We blew circles on the glass and wrote Down with McKinley in them. Then we headed home.

About halfway there, I said, "I didn't realize it was so far. Maybe we should've taken the bus."

"One dollar times two is two dollars," Al reminded me sternly. "That mounts up."

"Wait," I said and tied my sneaker.

"If he doesn't send me a birthday card, who cares?" Al said. "It's just a dumb old fourteenth birthday, anyway. Who cares?"

I didn't know if she meant her father or Brian. And I didn't ask.

chapter 7½

When I rang Al's bell next morning, she came to the door still in her pajamas, with a towel wrapped around her head.

"Are you doing needlepoint?" I said. Usually when she looks harassed that way it means she's doing needlepoint.

"No," she said grumpily. "I'm working my buns off. Come on in, but don't expect me to entertain you."

Entertain me? Since when. I followed her into her bedroom. It was a mess. It looked as if robbers had trashed it looking for cash stashed under the mattress. Or the world's biggest diamond.

"What happened?"

Al bent over a pile of clothes and began tossing them every which way. Bright spots of color flew through the air like confetti: yellow, red, blue, orange.

"I'm getting rid of it. Giving it all away."

I picked a plaid shirt off my head where it had landed. "What for?" I asked.

Al drew herself up and gave me her holy look. All she does to look holy, she told me, is think of St. Francis of Assisi feeding the starving pigeons. I've tried it on my mother when she's accused me of something I've done, or haven't done. It doesn't do any good at all. Al is a master of the holy look.

"I am divesting myself of my possessions," she said solemnly. I almost laughed. She *did* look funny. But in the nick of time I stopped. Laughter at that moment would've been the kiss of death.

"What for?" I asked again.

"The time has come for me to face up to the fact that I'm aging. My body is getting older, but my head remains static." Al frowned. "You know something? I'm a selfish person. I do nothing to justify my place on earth. I think too much of material things. And so do you."

Leave me out of it, I thought. I don't like it when Al drags me into her soul-searching. Let her search her own soul.

"Fourteen is a tremendous turning point," she continued. "Most people think sixteen or eighteen or twenty-one are the biggies. But I'm here to tell you fourteen is the most important birthday of all."

Al's been working up to this for a long time, I realized.

"It is?" was all I said.

"Do you realize in the Middle Ages a fourteen-year-old was considered a woman? That when Juliet was fourteen she was hanging out on the balcony wondering wherefore was Romeo? That Joan of Arc was fourteen when she heard the voices that led her into battle to save France?"

"Yeah, and look what happened to her." I couldn't resist. I had to put in my two cents.

I don't think Al heard me.

"That at fourteen," she went on, "Shirley Temple was already a millionaire?"

One minute we're talking Juliet and Joan of Arc. The next, we're onto Shirley Temple. Wild. Weird.

"The time has come to rid myself of my worldly goods," Al concluded, looking even more soulful.

"*All* your worldly goods?" I said.

Behind her glasses Al's eyes were huge and filled with life's mystery.

"All," she said, bowing her head.

"Can I have your lavender sweater, then?" I asked.

Al's eyes lost their soulful look.

"You are positively disgusting!" she snapped. "You make me ill. I shall give my lavender sweater to the poor and the needy. Along with everything else."

"How about your red shoes?" I had her. I knew I had her. She would never, never give up those red shoes. It would be like giving up her life.

Al thought a long minute. "Well," she conceded, "I might keep them. If only to remind myself of my former excesses. Besides," she said, "if you want to know, those shoes are very uncomfortable. No poor person would want them. I plan to hang them over my bed to remind me of my foolish youth."

"Well," I said, "it's going to be a big change, that's for sure."

"You have only one year left to be a child, my child." Al placed a hand gently on my shoulder. "Make the most of it." Then she started rooting around in her mess of clothing like a pig looking for truffles. "Scram," she said. "I have work to do."

I went to the door, opened it, took a step out into the hall. Then I hollered, "Your mother's going to have a cow!" slammed the door, and ran.

chapter 8

"I tell you what we *could* do." My mother threaded the needle with one eye closed, the only way she could do it, she said.

"Maybe they'll let you return my dress," I said, long-faced. "And give you back the five bucks."

She got it threaded on the third try. "I hate to sew," she murmured.

"Who would ever know?" I hate it when she starts to say something, then goes off on a tangent like that. "*What* could we do?"

"We could throw a birthday party for Al."

"Where?" I didn't tell her about Al renouncing

her worldly goods . . . I figured it would pass.

"Why, right here, of course. We could put the leaf in the table and polish the silver and have a cake with candles. Fourteen with one to grow on," my mother said, smiling at me.

"I don't know," I said. "Maybe Al wouldn't like a party right down the hall from where she lives."

"We could make it a surprise party," my mother said. Like most people, she hears what she wants to hear and throws the rest away.

"I don't think she'd be up for a surprise party. I think she'd flip if we all jumped out at her."

"We wouldn't jump out at her. We'd hide behind the door or someplace, and come out very casually. We could have balloons and party hats and . . ."

"Yeah, and little baskets filled with M and Ms," I added. "And we could play pin the tail on the donkey."

My mother gave me a long, hard stare.

"I hope you're not going into a difficult phase," she told me. "I understand some girls get rather impossible when they hit their teens. Somehow, I never thought it would happen to my little girl."

If there's one thing that sends me into a fit, it's being called my little girl, which my mother is fully aware of.

"Maybe I better sound Al out about this party," I suggested.

"That won't be necessary." My mother bit off a thread. "I'll simply call up and ask Al and her mother to come to dinner Saturday night."

"If you call Al on the telephone," I said, "she'll think somebody died. You've never called her in your entire life. She'll pass out."

Just then the hand of fate pressed our doorbell.

Two, then one, then two, the ring came.

"Ta dah!" Al breezed in under full sail, the *Niña*, the *Pinta*, and the *Santa María* all in one.

"Guess what? I just got a birthday card from my father. It was signed by Louise and all the boys. Can you beat it? It's a couple of days early, but my father said he wanted to be sure it arrived in time. There was a note from Louise. She said they hadn't been in touch because of having so many visitors. Her mother"—Al ticked off the visitors on her fingers—"and her brother and his wife, and some people she'd known when she lived in St. Louis. She said she hadn't had a minute to write. Also, Sam just got home from the hospital." Sam is Al's favorite stepbrother. Sam is beguiling, Al says. She's sappy about Sam.

"He had his appendix out," Al said. "Can you imagine a little guy like Sam being in the hospital? I bet he hated it. I thought people didn't even have their appendix out, anymore. I thought they left it in because it might come in handy someday."

"That's your tonsils, dumbo," I said. "If your appendix wants out, let it out. Polly had appendicitis and she said it hurt."

"The birthday card says, 'Present follows,' in my father's writing. What do you suppose they sent me? Maybe a pair of sweat pants to go with my sweat shirt. Then I'd have a total outfit." Al liked the idea, I could see.

"Yeah, pants with AL(exandra) the Great written all across your rear end," I said. "So they'd know who you are, coming and going."

Al's face was wreathed in smiles as she waited for me to finish talking so she could go on with what was on her mind. I know Al. Now that she'd heard from her father and Louise and the boys, she was on the glory road.

"Who needs a birthday party, anyway? Who cares? The Rainbow Room's not so much, anyway. Who cares?" She was a new woman.

"I do," my mother said. "A birthday party is in the cards for you, Al. I feel it in my bones."

"You do?" Al looked from me to my mother and back to me. She knew something was up.

"You're invited to a birthday party here, Saturday night," my mother told Al. "Just tell us whom you'd like to invite, and we'll invite them."

"Well." Al was flabbergasted, knocked out of her socks. I'd never seen her like this before and found it a real treat. She didn't know what to say.

"That's very nice of you," she settled on at last. "But won't it be a lot of trouble?"

"Everyone will pitch in," my mother said, in a soothing tone.

They will? My father could push the vacuum and Teddy could get down on his knees and attack the ring in the bathtub, a first for that little creep. My mother and I would prepare the food. Neato.

"Tell your mother I'll call her tonight," my mother told Al, "and let her know the plans. Better still, have her call me when she gets in, if she's not too tired."

Al and I zapped into my room for privacy.

"We were going to have it be a surprise," I said, "but I figured you'd freak out if we jumped out at you."

"I would have died," Al said. "I'm not up for surprises. What will I wear? I have nothing to wear!"

That's just what you get for giving away your worldly goods, I thought, but did not say.

"Just wear any old thing. Your denim skirt would be great with that nice blouse you have," I told her. "It doesn't matter."

"Yes, it does. If your mother's throwing me a party, I owe her the courtesy of dressing up," Al said solemnly.

"You know what?"

"No, what?"

"For a minute there, I thought your mother had snuck in. I thought it was your mother saying what you just said. You sounded just like her."

"Yikes!" Al clutched her head. "What a terrible thing to say!"

chapter 9

"Hello, Daddy." My mother was on the horn, talking to her father. They talk a couple of times a week. My grandfather lives alone. My mother worries about him being lonely. My father says how can he be lonely with all those luscious ladies inviting him for potluck?

"You'd think he was rich," my father teases my mother. "Maybe he better let those gals know he's not. I wish your father would let me in on his secret." My grandfather has the reputation of being a ladies' man.

My grandmother died when I was five months old. My mother says I was a great comfort to her after her mother died. She'd hold me and walk around the apartment with me in her arms, and it made her feel better, she says. Less sad.

"A baby is a lovely thing," my mother told me, "especially when someone you love very much dies. A baby is a new soul, a fresh new soul to take the place of the person who's died." I like that idea.

When she tells what a comfort I was to her when I was five months old, Teddy gets very jealous. He wants to know why she couldn't have held him to make her feel better. The fact that he wasn't born yet doesn't seem to occur to him. I hope Teddy gets smarter as he gets older, the way you're supposed to, but I wouldn't put any money on it.

"We're having a birthday party for Al on Saturday," I heard her say. "You remember Al, don't you? Yes, that's the one. Well, she's going to be fourteen so we thought . . . yes, why, that would be wonderful. I'm sure the girls would love it. It starts at seven. Grand. Good-bye, darling." My mother calls her father Daddy and darling. I like to hear her call him things like that. I think when I'm middle-aged and my father is old, I'll do the same.

"Amazing!" my mother said when she'd hung up. "Absolutely amazing. Grandfather wants to come to Al's party."

"He's not bringing Mrs. Oakley, is he?" I asked. Mrs. Oakley came to our apartment the day Teddy sang the dirty song. The same day Al and I hid in the broom closet while Teddy performed, we were so embarrassed. My mother told me later that Mrs. Oakley kept time to the music with her dainty foot and never turned a hair at Teddy's lyrics.

"You've got to give the old girl credit," my father said. He likes Mrs. Oakley. My mother can take her or leave her.

"He's coming alone," my mother said. "I would never have thought of asking him, but he's fond of Al."

"Al thinks Grandfather's an ace," I said.

My mother laughed. "And so he is," she agreed.

"So that makes you and Dad, me and Al, Al's mother, Polly, and Grandfather," I counted on my fingers. "Seven in all."

"Don't forget Teddy," my mother tossed out, leaving the room on the pretext of work to be done. She was escaping from me, I'm sure of it.

No, sir. I put my foot down on Teddy. In more ways than one. Teddy would have to be eliminated. For the evening. Nothing permanent. Ha, ha.

We haven't discussed the menu yet. If my mother says tuna or meat loaf, the party's off. Polly said she'd bake a cake. Al's mother called and was almost crying, she was so delighted about us giving Al a party.

"You have no idea what your family means to us," Al's mother told mine. "You've made us feel right at home here and more of a family together, Al and me. I can never thank you enough. This will be a memorable occasion."

Not if we have tuna-fish surprise it won't be.

But I underestimated my mother. She decided to spring

for a standing rib roast. And it wasn't even on special! My father's eyes misted over as he heard the news.

"When was the last time we had a rib roast?" he said wistfully. "Wasn't it the day you told me you were having a baby? And that," he pointed to me, "was the baby, and she's about to be thirteen. I'm pretty sure that was the last time we had a rib roast."

My mother looked at him in a way that, if Al had looked that way, it would've been a super duper piercer.

"And I think asparagus would be nice." My mother plowed onward.

On my mother's family's coat of arms is engraved, "Never buy fresh fruit or vegetables out of season." This was going to be a bang-up bash, all right.

Just as we were discussing what flavor ice cream might be best, the bell rang. Two, then one, then two. It was the guest of honor, two days early.

I opened the door a crack. "Go away," I said. "You've got the wrong night."

"Ta dah!" Al stood there in her red shoes, her AL(exandra) the Great T-shirt, and a billowy skirt that reached her ankles. She was smiling. "I think I've got it," she said softly. "I really think I've got it this time."

"Got what?" I whispered, afraid of breaking the spell.

Al looked over her left shoulder, then over her right. When she saw the coast was clear, she whispered, "Zandi."

Was this the secret password?

"How do you spell it?" I asked.

"With a capital Z," she said, "and an *i* at the end. How does that grab you?"

"Well," I opened the door all the way, "it's different. I'll say that. The trouble is, with an unusual name like Zandi, nobody will know how to spell it. You'll get it spelled all kinds of ways. It's sort of far out, you might say."

"That's what I like about it." Al couldn't stop smiling. "This morning, when I woke up, a little voice said, right smack in my ear, it said, 'Your name is Zandi.' Just like that." Al looked closely at me to see if I bought that one. I kept my face inscrutable, which ain't easy.

"So then I hopped out of bed," Al continued, "and looked in the mirror, and, sure enough, I looked like a Zandi.

"And you know something?" Al scrunched up her face. "It's perfect. I feel it in my bones, and my bones never lie."

"You'll be the first in your crowd with that name," I told her. "That's for sure."

I swung the door back and forth, wanting to tell Al about the rib roast and the asparagus and figuring this wasn't the right time.

"You want me to start calling you that now?" I said. "Before your birthday, I mean?"

"That's OK," Al said. "You can wait until the big day. I have to keep saying it to myself to make it seem real, though."

And I watched as she walked down the hall and let herself into her apartment, repeating, "Zandi, Zandi," over and over, until she got the hang of it.

chapter 10

"My mother's bringing the horses doovries," Al announced.

"The what?"I said.

"You know, the stuff you eat with drinks before you get down to the serious eating," Al explained. "She does this thing with pineapple and cream cheese and curry powder."

I looked at her.

"The first time she made it," Al continued, "I pulled a boo-boo. I pretended I liked it. My mother's no ace in the kitchen, as you know, and she needs reinforcement when it comes to her culinary efforts." Al gave me a piercer. "From here on in, kid, take Mother Al's advice. Tell it like it is. If it's gross, say it's gross. Even if it hurts. In the long run, the truth will out. It cuts down on the pineapple and curry-powder jazz."

She proceeded to pace, wearing a path on the already worn rug. "So do me a favor, OK? Pretend you like it. Even if it makes you want to barf. So she doesn't get hurt feelings."

"Sure, Mother Al. Whatever you say. But I thought your name was Mother Zandi." I couldn't help giggling. I could see Al dressed in a purple turban, bending over her crystal ball. In a deep, dark voice I said, "Beware the ides of September, Mother Zandi. Watch out for a tall, bald man, smoking a fat black cigar and carrying a teddy bear on his back."

Al took it up.

"I, Mother Zandi," she began in an even deeper and darker voice, "advise on all matters in life. There is no problem Mother Zandi cannot solve. I can tell you the color of your aura and warn of good and bad cycles you must pass through before you come out on the other side without harm."

"What? Color of my aura?"

Al nodded, looking wise, if weary. "The atmosphere that emanates from any and all bodies," she said.

I looked down at myself, at my body. Nothing.

"I don't think I have an aura," I told her.

She raised her eyes to the ceiling. "All mortals have an aura. Perhaps yours is concealed beneath your skin and will show itself only when you reach puberty. Upon the receipt of certain fees, I, Mother Zandi, will reveal to you the color of your aura when the right moment arrives." Al pulled down her bangs as far as they'd go and glared at me. "When Mother Zandi speaks, the world trembles," she intoned.

"It's a good thing you changed your name," I said. "Mother Zandi sounds classy, like the real thing, and Mother Al sounds like a new health-food line. Mother Al's Tofu would be good. Or how about Mother Al's Bulgar?"

"I'm glad your grandfather's coming to the party." Al spun off on another tack. "I think it's really cool of him to want to come. You didn't threaten him with anything to make him come, did you?"

"Of course not," I said. "He likes you. My mother didn't even think to invite him. He invited himself."

"That's really nice. I mean, a man of his age probably doesn't get asked to too many birthday parties. Probably most of his friends have retired to Florida or have died off," Al said.

"Hey, he isn't that old. He's only sixty-six," I said.

"A mere boy. What do you think we ought to plan for after dinner? Do you think we should play games or just talk?" Al pondered what to do after dinner, something I hadn't thought of. "Maybe we could have a stimulating conversation," she said, frowning. "An exchange of ideas, discussing the latest books, the latest plays we've seen. How about that?"

"The latest book I read was *Misty of Chincoteague*," I said. "And my grandfather took me to see *Cats*. We could zero in on *Cats*. Is that what you meant?"

"You are such a turkey." Al sighed. "We have here a classic case of youth and age. And ne'er the twain shall meet. How about if we played bridge?"

"I don't know how," I said. "Do you?"

"My mother tried to teach me and I freaked. You have to remember all the cards that have been played, and keep track of the cards in other peoples' hands. It's a real drag, if you ask me," Al said. "How about *vingt et un?*"

"Or better yet," said I, "crazy eights."

"You make it awfully hard to get off the ground," Al told me in a cross tone. "After all, your grandfather's a man of the world. I can just see him, dressed in an opera cape and top hat, drinking champagne out of some showgirl's slipper." A small smile creased Al's face. "I can see him cruising through Central Park at midnight in a horse-drawn carriage. His companion has skin like milk and wears diamonds around her throat, her wrist and her ankles. She has on so many diamonds she clanks when she moves." Al got up and imitated the showgirl decorated with diamonds.

"And following your grandfather's horse-drawn carriage, in hot pursuit," Al stomped her feet loudly, "is another horse-drawn carriage bearing a jealous suitor of your grandfather's companion. He is tailing them to their tryst and plans on challenging your grandfather to a duel."

"I don't think my grandfather was even alive when they challenged people to duels," I said.

But, oblivious to my protests, Al crossed her hands on her chest, and with a soulful expression on her face she broke into "Ah, Sweet Mystery of Life," which she'd picked up from some late late movie starring Nelson Eddy and Jeanette MacDonald.

When she'd finished and, exhausted, slumped onto my bed, I said, "There's always Monopoly," but Al only sighed deeply and said, "Oh, to have been young when men were men and women weren't liberated."

Then she sat up suddenly.

"But, when you come right down to it," Al's eyes flashed angrily, "who wants some nerd drinking champagne out of their shoe? Brian would never do such a dumb thing."

How come we always wound up back at the same old place, Brian city?

"Yeah," I said, giving her a wide yawn, "they'd probably throw him out of the 4-H Club if he did."

chapter 11

At dusk my mother and I watched the outbound traffic clog the streets. It was the start of Labor Day weekend and, like lemmings fleeing to the sea, the cars were fleeing to the country. The horizon wore a stripe of pale orange, which might mean rain. From where we stood at the window on the fourteenth floor we could barely hear the horns blaring, and the cars looked harmless, even quaint.

"Thank God we're not among them," my father said fervently, on his way to the kitchen to make his special horseradish sauce. When he'd gone, I said to my mother, "What about Teddy?"

"Oh, he'll be fine," she said in a vague way. My mother

is hardly ever vague, and when she is, watch out. It means trouble.

"Whayda mean, he'll be fine? Where's he staying while the party's on?"

"Here," my mother said. "And Hubie will be here to keep him company." With that, she skimmed across the room, away from me. I skimmed after her.

"What gives?" I asked. "I thought you were farming Teddy out. Now we get Hubie thrown in for bad measure. *Quel* bummer." I clutched my head, expecting no sympathy, which was good, as none was forthcoming.

"They'll be fine," my mother said. "I'll feed them early, and we'll move the television into our room so they can watch it there. Hubie's mother asked if he could stay here since she has out-of-town visitors and needs all the beds. She's done so many favors for me I couldn't refuse. Don't worry." She patted my shoulder. "It will be a grand party. One to make you proud. One Al will always remember."

"How could you let this happen, God?" I asked.

"Beats me," Teddy piped up.

I swung at him and missed. My hand grazed the wall. I yelped, and Teddy grinned and fled. I escaped down the hall.

I rang Al's bell three times. They must be out. Just when I had about given up, the door opened slowly. A disembodied hand bearing a small square of white crept toward me. It said, "Mother Zandi, Swami. By appt. only."

"I have an appointment," I said in a loud voice. The door creaked open farther. Al had painted a huge, gleaming red mouth over her own pale lips. Her eyes, ringed with mascara, peered blearily out at me. A black satin turban hid all her hair, except for a couple of wisps of bangs. When she smiled I saw her mouth had leaked onto her teeth and made them pink. She looked about fifty years old.

"Enter," she said in a swami voice. "Mother Zandi says watch for false friends today. Mother Zandi also says do not spend money you don't have, as this leads to bankruptcy."

"Hey, I know all that," I said. "I was just coming up for air. It's getting pretty hairy at home. You look great. Not a day over thirteen and a half."

"Come in, my child, and we will sit in the hot tub for a spell." I followed Al inside. The living room was dim, curtains drawn. Candles sputtered on a table.

"You are some nut," I said.

"Disrespect of Mother Zandi will lead to mayhem," she whispered. "Mother Zandi's bunions are buzzing, and she must sit down. Sit with me, and I will tell you your future."

The doorbell rang. We both jumped.

"Sign here," the delivery boy said, looking at his pad. When Al signed, he handed over the long thin bundle.

"What is it?" Al said.

"Flowers. By Vivian. 'Every posy a poem,' Viv says. But these days who knows? Maybe it's a cobra lying inside waiting for you weirdos to unwrap him so's he can take a chomp on you. Have a good day," and he tipped his hat and whistled his way to the elevator.

We zapped inside and laid the package on the table.

"I think I saw it move," I said.

"Smell it," Al suggested.

"What does a cobra smell like?"

"Like any old snake. Here." Al slit the wrapping open with a scissors. A dozen long-stemmed roses lay inside.

Al picked out the card and read, "Sorry to miss the party. All love, Stan."

"Oh, boy," Al said. "What does 'All love' mean? Is that the same as 'All my love,' or does it go deeper than that?"

"I have to split," I said. "My mother will be combing the bullrushes for me. Have a good day, like the man said."

"Have a weird day, comrade," Al told me, and filled a vase with water for the roses.

chapter 12

A party is always more work than you think it'll be. My mother whirled around like a dervish, my father worked on his horseradish sauce, aiming for perfection. Teddy twisted his hair into corkscrews, the way he does when he's coming down with something, and made listless passes at the freezer compartment, threatening to start in on the ice cream. Just before six, the bell rang. It was the same delivery boy who'd delivered the roses to Al's mother.

"Hey," he said when he saw me, "long time no see. More posies from Viv." It was a centerpiece for the table from Al's mother. My mother stood back to admire it and said she'd never seen anything so exquisite.

"I think I oughta be videotaped," Teddy whined, conscious of losing center stage.

"What for?" I asked.

"On account of if anybody ever kidnaps me they'll know how to find me if I'm videotaped. I saw it on TV. Hubie says he's already been videotaped."

"Anybody ever kidnaps you, kid," I reassured him, "they'll have you back within the hour. Don't worry about a thing."

My mother rested her cheek against the back of Teddy's neck. "He hasn't got a fever," she said, "but he looks flushed."

"It's all the excitement," my father said.

The doorbell rang again, and I said, "more posies from Viv, probably." But it was Al. Cheeks flaming, she wore her party dress, brand-new for the big event. "She just gave it to me," Al said.

"We'll almost be twins," I told her. Her dress was a lot like mine except that it had blue stripes instead of black, and different sleeves.

"I love the way it whispers when I walk," I said. "It makes me feel like Scarlett O'Hara."

"Yeah, well, mine makes me feel like Rhett Butler," Al told me. But I could tell from the way her eyes sparkled she felt good in her new dress. "And frankly, my dear," Al went on, "I don't give a you-know-what."

"What's you-know-what mean?" Teddy asked.

"Next time *Gone with the Wind*'s on the tube, Ted,

catch it and you'll find out. I'm not allowed to swear around the junior jet set."

"In October," Teddy bragged, "I'm hitting the double digits. I'm gonna be ten. When you go from nine to ten, you hit the double digits."

"Right you are," Al said. "Going from nine to ten is almost as earth-shaking as going from thirteen to fourteen."

"And going from forty to fifty is even more earthshaking," my father said. "How's the birthday girl, Al? Do we call you Alexandra now? No more Al, I bet. You're getting too sophisticated for Al, so Alexandra it is."

Al gave me a piercer and mouthed, "You told!" at me.

"I did not," I protested. "He thought that up all by himself."

"Thought what up?" my father asked. The bell rang again, and this time it was Hubie. Backpack, hiking boots, and all.

"Come on in, Spiderman," I told Hubie.

Hubie's blond hair flopped into his blue eyes. His sweet, rosy little mouth smiled, and his dimples danced. Hubie was a terror.

"Don't anybody sit down," my mother warned. "I just plumped up all the down cushions and everything's perfect. Leave it that way."

"What's for supper, Mom?" Teddy asked.

"Hamburgers for you two."

"I had hamburgers for lunch," came from Hubie.

"I thought your mother doesn't believe in meat," Teddy said.

"She changed her mind," said Hubie.

Al headed for the door. "I better go home and get doozied up," she said.

"I thought you *were* doozied up," my father told her.

"I am, but I'm not finished yet."

"You wearing those shoes?" Teddy asked, showing off for Hubie. Al had on her clunky red shoes. "I thought they made your behind wiggle," Teddy said. He and Hubie broke into gales of laughter. Al blushed furiously. Teddy must've overheard Al and me talking about her red shoes, which did sometimes make her behind wiggle, but it was certainly none of Teddy's business.

"Get lost, troglodyte," I said, and he and Hubie disappeared, probably to lay plans to blow up the Statue of Liberty.

The bell rang again. When I answered, the same old delivery boy said, "Hey, fate throws us together once more," and thrust yet another bouquet of posies from Vivian into my hands.

"They're for you, Al," I said. The delivery boy, feeling, by now, like an old friend of the family, stepped inside, leaned over my shoulder to read the card, and said, "Yeah, from somebody named Stan."

"Holy Toledo," Al said softly, looking slightly fuzzy around the edges, "and the party hasn't even begun."

"This guy Stan really knows how to overdo it, doesn't he?" I said.

"Yeah, he sure does," Al said, smiling. "But he overdoes in such a tasteful way, *n'est-ce-pas?*"

chapter 13

Polly arrived at six-thirty, carrying the cake, which was done up to resemble an Egyptian mummy. "I took a cab," Polly told us, " 'cause I was afraid it might get crushed on the bus."

Slowly, slowly, she peeled off the layers of tin foil and plastic wrap. We all stood silent, tongue-tied in admiration.

The cake must've had three layers, maybe more. Every inch was covered with a magnificent dark-chocolate frosting. Polly had decorated it with hearts and flowers and squiggles. AL IS FOURTEEN was written in pale pink icing.

It was a work of art.

"We won't eat it," my father said. "We'll put it under glass." We broke up, as if he'd said something hysterically funny. Excitement was high. It wasn't every day we gave a birthday party for Al, every day we had a rib roast in the oven, every day we had Al's mother coming to our house for dinner. My grandfather arrived shortly before seven. He had a present for Al, but he wouldn't tell me what it was. We were giving her a little black suede shoulder bag with a tiny rhinestone clasp. I would've loved such a bag. I never go anywhere, but still.

At five past seven, the doorbell rang. It wasn't Al's special ring, so I thought, Oh, no, more flowers. But there they were: Al and her mother. Al looked beautiful. Her hair was off her forehead and swept to one side. She looked about sixteen. Her cheeks flamed, her eyes shone, her feet wouldn't stay still. She had on black suede shoes with little heels. They would be perfect with the bag. She had on panty hose, and they didn't even wrinkle at the ankles. She looked *soignée*. When we got a minute alone, I'd tell her so.

Al's mother, dressed in a floaty red dress, also looked *soignée*, but then she always does. Al stood aside to let her mother enter first. Al's mother smelled delicious. She must've taken a bath.

Why? Is one missing?

That was one of my father's golden oldie jokes.

Did you take a bath? No, is one missing? The things they laughed at, back in the dark ages!

As Al, guest of honor, followed her mother into our

living room, I heard her say, so softly only I could hear, "Ta dah!" That almost broke me up.

Polly was a tremendous guest, small-talking with the oldsters like a real pro. And I was proud of my grandfather. He looked positively ambassadorial in his striped suit that, he told me once, he wore only to weddings and funerals. Well, this was neither. As Al pointed out, he probably didn't get invited to too many birthday parties. At his age.

Everybody, including me, I thought smugly, looked elegant. Except Teddy, who was chained to the TV set with his buddy, Hubie. At first everybody also seemed to be moving in slow motion, like in a dream. Then they relaxed. The grown-ups had drinks while Polly, Al, and I slurped iced tea. I watched Al watching her mother out of the corner of her eye. She wanted her mother to have a good time and get along with my parents. That's only natural. When you have a best friend, you always want her mother to get along with yours. It's very unrealistic, however, to think that your parents and your friend's parents will socialize. The chances of them having anything in common are about zilch. Still, it would be nice if they did.

I was interested to see that Al's mother was slightly on edge at first. I didn't know that grown-ups sometimes become unraveled, just the way kids do, in a new and strange situation. I thought all grown-ups were cool. But I could tell she wasn't quite comfortable. Not at first, that is. And my own mother and father were also slightly off kilter. It was Polly and my grandfather who pulled things together. Both of them were real pros: Polly because she'd led such a sophisticated life—traveled so much and lived in lots of exotic places. And my grandfather because he was a kind man, a real gentleman, who knew how to make people comfortable. My mother, I knew, was worried about the dinner turning out right, and my father was the host and so preoccupied with his job of filling glasses and passing things that he couldn't be totally concerned with the guests.

My grandfather liked Al's mother. I could tell. Every time she said something, he gave her his complete attention, leaning toward her, his eyes on her face. He made her feel like a star, I think. I'd never seen my grandfather with a total stranger before. Only with Mrs. Oakley, whom he'd known a while, as well as with other people he'd known for some time. He'd only just met Al's mother. What a scene. I loved it. Once I caught Al looking at her mother and my grandfather, and she was smiling. Her mother was having a good time, and that made her happy.

After a certain amount of scurrying back and forth to the kitchen to check on things, my mother announced dinner was served. Not only did we have candles and flowers and linen napkins and tablecloth and roast beef, we also had place cards. That was my idea. I thought place cards were the cat's meow. It was like being at the palace when you had place cards. I don't know *what* palace, exactly, but you know what I mean.

My mother had me do the place cards, since my handwriting is much better than hers. When I go slowly, take my time, mine's quite classy. Hers is like chicken tracks.

Despite the place cards, my mother said, "You're here, Virginia," to Al's mother. I didn't know she even knew what Al's mother's name was. "And Dad, you're next to Virginia. Polly, dear, will you sit here, please, and Al, you're here." My mother indicated the chair next to my father.

Out in the kitchen, I hissed, "Don't you think Al should open her presents now?"

"No," my mother hissed back. "After dinner. More festive."

The rib roast was carried out with ceremony. And reigned like a visiting dignitary. The little roasted new potatoes, which I'd coated with my finely chopped parsley, plus the asparagus, brought forth a chorus of oooohs and ahs. Even Polly looked impressed. My father's special horseradish sauce, heaped into a little silver bowl, was splendid.

My father said grace, as he always does. Then everyone drank a toast to Al's health and happiness and continued longevity. "And may you always be as happy as right at this minute, Al," my father told her. Al blushed. The dinner commenced. My father began to carve. Slice after slice of the beef, paper thin and done to the perfect shade of pink, fell under his knife.

I can't exactly explain, but it was beautiful. All the vibes were good. It was one of those perfect times you remember. Al talked and laughed, and once or twice I caught her just sitting still, looking around the table at all the faces, all of us gathered here in her honor. Maybe she was thinking of her father, wishing he and his gang were all here. Maybe she wished Brian was here, too. Anyway, it was great.

Polly and I cleared the salad plates. We wouldn't let Al help. Then we put the presents in front of Al. She looked a little embarrassed to be the cynosure of all eyes.

"This will give you a chance to work up an appetite for the ice cream and cake, Al," my mother said. My father tapped a spoon against his glass and said, "Hear ye, hear ye," and Al opened her presents. Ours came first. She nearly went ape. "I've never had one like this!" she gasped, and got up and kissed my mother and father, saying, "Thanks, thanks." For one awful moment, I was afraid she might kiss me, too. But she didn't.

My grandfather gave her a copy of *You Know Me Al*, a book by Ring Lardner, which he'd mentioned to Al the first time he met her. She loved that. Her mother gave her a birthday card with a check inside. "Oh, Ma, you already gave me the dress," Al said. Al's mother busied herself with a handkerchief, careful of her mascara. The long thin package done up in brown paper with Al's name and address on it turned out to be from Louise and Al's father and the boys. It was a needlepoint picture Louise had done of the farm, with the family members lined up: Al's father, Louise, Nick, Chris, and Sam. And Al.

"See! That's me, on the right, the tall one," Al said gleefully. "Louise did it all by herself." She read the enclosed note. "Isn't that clever of her! It's all of us in Ohio. Isn't that too much!"

I think that needlepoint picture was her favorite present. Al's mother was a good sport. If Al's obvious enthusiasm for the picture hurt her, she didn't let on.

Polly not only made Al's cake, she also gave her a length of material from Africa, which, Polly said, could be worn as a dress or a sarong or anything you chose. She'd show Al how to wind it around herself, Polly promised.

We put fifteen candles (one to grow on) on the cake. Al blew them out in one breath as we sang "Happy Birthday to You." Her wish will come true. We had vanilla, as well as mocha chocolate-chip ice cream. I took vanilla because I was afraid we'd run out of mocha chocolate chip. Al ate slowly. Eating slowly cuts down on caloric intake, she told me.

After, we played charades. My grandfather was hysterical acting out the Hunchback of Notre Dame. Al's mother stood staring at the ceiling, hands clasped, supposedly Joan of Arc. No one guessed her. My mother acted out Charlie Chaplin as the Little Tramp. My father got to do Marilyn Monroe. He walked around with his mouth half open and his eyes half closed. He was a riot. Polly acted out Julia Child. I guessed her right away. I was Abraham Lincoln. I pretended I'd been shot, and staggered around quite a lot. Al said I should've given the Gettysburg Address. I hate know-it-alls, I told her, even if it was her birthday.

Al got a tough one to act out: the Wizard of Oz. She gazed into an imaginary crystal ball. I was the only one who knew what she was doing. Nobody guessed her.

My grandfather took Polly home in a taxi. Al and her mother thanked us many times. "I've never enjoyed an evening more in my life," Al's mother said, pressing cheeks with my mother.

"All I can say is," Al said, "this party makes the Rainbow Room look like the Automat." Then they left. My mother slipped her shoes off and lay down on the sofa. The bell rang. "Who on earth is that?" my mother said, slipping her shoes back on.

"She forgot this." Al handed me a tray with a large stuffed pineapple reclining upon it. "The horses doovries. My mother says forgive her, she's so embarrassed she forgot it. Good night and thanks again."

"What's that?" my father asked, coming out of the kitchen, pointing at the pineapple.

"It's Al's mother's horses doovries," I explained. "She forgot them."

"Too bad," said my father, circling the pineapple as if it were a live hand grenade.

"Say what you will," my mother said, "those little boys were wonderful. Not a peep out of them."

Speak of the devil. Wearing pajamas and a fuzzy look, Hubie staggered in. "I think I'm walking in my sleep," he mumbled. "Where's the cake?"

"Where's Teddy?" my mother said. "Asleep?"

"He's sick. He told me to bring him a piece of cake. So here I am." Hubie dug at his eyes with his fists.

"Sick?" My mother and father looked startled.

"He's got spots."

"Where?"

"All over."

My mother and father rushed toward Teddy's room.

"It's probably early acne," I said.

"Either that or measles. Probably measles." Hubie shrugged. He didn't give up easily. "Where's the cake?" he said again.

chapter 14

"Teddy has chicken pox," I told Al the next day. "Talk about timing. Just before school starts. The kid's a genius."

"The kid's also gonna itch like fury," Al said. We were walking to Rockefeller Center to watch the tourists hang out and to talk to Rudy.

He had told us holidays were a perfect time to play his violin in tourist haunts. "Strolling violinists are in short supply back in Keokuk," he said. "Those of my caliber, anyway. They love me, they think I'm Mr. New York. Little do they know I was born in Jersey City."

"You said you were born on a roller coaster at Coney

Island," I reminded him. "Right," he snapped his fingers. "It was my twin brother was born in Jersey City." There's no way to keep up with him. He's a card.

"The dinner was delicious," Al told me, stomping along. For once she left her red shoes home. She wore her running shoes, instead. "My mother had a super time. I'll remember that party until the day I die. Maybe longer."

"It was fun," I agreed. "We had a great time."

"First let's check out the place we saw that woman," Al said. "I have some money today. I can't cash my birthday check on Sunday, but my mother gave me an advance on it. I'm giving that poor soul five dollars to buy food for her family."

"Let's find Rudy first," I said. I didn't want to see that woman again. I was afraid of her. I don't know why, but I was. I have a bad habit of postponing things I don't want to face.

"What's with you?" Al asked, puzzled. "You want to forget her, don't you?"

"Not forget exactly," I said. "I can't exactly explain. She scares me."

"Then you must be scared a lot. There're a lot of starving people around these days. You might say it's an epidemic. She must be weak as a cat." Al scowled at me. "What could she do to you?"

"I'm not scared of what she might do." I tried to explain. "I'm scared of what she might say, how she'd look at me."

Al set the pace. We walked briskly at first, until the

heat got to be too much. Then we slowed down, pacing ourselves.

"I love the city on holidays. It's almost like the country." Al flung wide her arms, indicating the almost deserted streets, the absence of traffic. "All we need are a few cows and a couple of pigs and we're in clover." Then she cried, "Look, isn't that Rudy?"

"Where?" I squinted and couldn't see anyone who looked like Rudy.

"There. Sure that's him. Hey, Rudy!" Al hollered.

A young couple in front of us, each walking hand in hand with a small child, jumped and looked back at us apprehensively. They must've thought we were New York weirdos.

"Come on, let's cross. I'm sure it's him."

When we got to where Rudy should've been, he wasn't there. "I told you it wasn't him," I said crossly. "It's too hot to run. Let's sit down, if we can find a place." But the benches lining the walkway to the skating rink were filled with people eating Italian ices or sandwiches from home.

We never got a seat, and we never found Rudy. After a long while we headed east to find the woman. Al wouldn't let me off the hook.

"You're an escapist," she told me sternly. "You don't want to face reality."

"Look who's talking," I snapped.

There was no one standing under the clock at the bank. The temperature was 81°, the time 11:32.

"Let's go home," I started to say.

"There she is," Al told me. "Coming toward us."

"That's not her."

"Sure it is." Al fumbled in her pocket.

The woman approached, head down, shuffling, looking at the sidewalk. A kid about Teddy's age was with her. I couldn't tell if it was a boy or a girl. It didn't matter. The kid's hair and clothes were matted with filth. They both wore pieces of shoes tied with string. The kid stopped, picked something out of a trash basket, looked at it, tossed it aside.

Her skin was the same ruddy color. I couldn't see the eyes. The hand came out, as if by accident, as we came abreast; the fingernails curved, the fingers bloated and swollen, as the other's had been. I put a quarter timidly in the hand. And swiftly moved on.

"Hssst!" The sound commanded me to stop, to turn, to look at her. It wasn't the same person. I had known all along. These eyes were dark and full of hate. I had never seen so much hate. She spit at me, mumbled something terrible. I made myself forget what she said. I began to walk fast. Then I was running.

I ran until my beating heart forced me to stop. I leaned against a building, waiting for Al. If she didn't show, I'd go home alone. If she didn't show, maybe something bad had happened.

With a huge surge of relief, I saw her coming at last. I took long, deep breaths to calm myself until she caught up. As we headed up Lexington, we were both shaking.

I made myself look straight ahead, neither to the left nor the right. For fear of what I might see.

"Listen," Al said, "it could happen to anyone."

"It wasn't the same woman," I said flatly. "And you know it."

We cut across Seventy-second Street. The digital clock on the corner said it was 12:06.

Almost time for lunch.

chapter 15

"So you were right. Big deal." Al stomped her way around the rug. "So we'll try again." She meant try to find the woman, give her the money.

"Count me out," I said. "Last night I had a horrible dream. It was night and I was walking down a scrungy little side street, with garbage cans lining either side. It smelled. There was no moon, no stars, nothing. Only me. I thought I heard someone following me, so I walked faster. Just as I got to the end of the street, I was surrounded. They were all women and they all looked alike, just like the woman we saw yesterday. They were making dog noises low in their throats, mumbling terrible things.

Then they closed in on me. I hollered and screamed, and nobody came." As I told Al my dream, my heart started to pound, it was so real.

"So then they caught me and tied me to a post. And boy, did they smell!" I grabbed my nose and pinched it to illustrate how bad they smelled. "They started throwing rocks at me. Then they lit a fire." I felt the back of my nose getting scratchy and knew I was going to cry.

"Excuse me," I said, and fled to the bathroom. Al pulls that one on me all the time. Now it was my turn.

When I came back, Al hadn't moved.

"Know something?"

"No," I said.

"Your grandfather asked my mother out."

I started laughing.

"What's so funny?" Al's face got red.

"Nothing. It's just that it was such a drastic subject change." I couldn't stop laughing. Al's face got redder.

When I got hold of myself, I said, "You're kidding!"

Al drew herself up haughtily.

"Why would I kid you about something as serious as that?" she demanded. "And why do you find it so impossible that your grandfather would ask my mother to go to the ballet? My mother has men ask her to go all sorts of places. She never lacks for dates, as you well know."

"Come off it, Al," I said. "I think my grandfather showed very good taste asking your mother out. It's just that I'm surprised. Is she going?"

"She thinks your grandfather's a charming man. She told me she's seldom met a more charming man. Of course she's going. She loves the ballet."

"How about Stan?" I couldn't resist asking.

"Oh, well," Al waved her hands in the air, "Stan's still in Europe. Anyway, they're just good friends."

I almost reminded Al that she said her mother might marry Stan and they'd move to a mansion in the suburbs. But I didn't. No sense in rocking the boat.

"I think that's cool," I told her. "Your mother and my grandfather going on a date. Maybe we could go along as chaperones."

"Two people of their age hardly need chaperones," Al said, in an icy tone.

"Hey, I was only kidding," I said.

"How old is your grandfather, anyway?"

"Sixty-six. How old's your mother?"

"I'm not sure. Either forty-four or forty-five. Sometimes she forgets what year she was born." Al looked at the ceiling, doing a little arithmetic in her head. "He's old enough to be her father," she said.

"Sure. He's my mother's father, and she's forty-one."

Al thought that one over and found nothing there to quibble about. She got up, pulled herself together, and made for the door.

"Gotta split now," she announced. "I have to write a letter."

"To Brian?"

"No, to your mother. To thank her for the super party. See you."

I could hardly wait for my mother to come home to tell her about Al's mother and Grandfather. I was brat-sitting, carrying shooters of Coke to Teddy as he lay swilling them down on his bed of pain.

"I'm thirsty!" he bellowed for about the twentieth time. And although it was the middle of the day, I went into the bathroom, locked the door, and turned on the shower, hard, so I couldn't hear Teddy or anyone else, and took a long, hot shower to cool myself off.

chapter 16

"Do you realize," Al spoke deliberately, pronouncing each word with great solemnity, "that when Joan of Arc was little more than our age, she was leading the armies of France against the English and raising the siege of Orlé-ans?" I felt her giving me a piercer and thought, Oh, boy, it's going to be one of those days.

Al was all wound up. We were on our way to meet Polly. The three of us planned one last blast before school started the next day.

"I've decided I lead a totally useless life. I mean, what do I do to help mankind?"

I knew Al didn't expect an answer from me. Which was a good thing.

"You lead a totally useless life, too," she told me.

That was pretty nervy of her. It's OK if she wants to say *she* leads a totally useless life. That's her affair. But she doesn't have to include me. I clean and cook and iron napkins. Now and then. This year I'm planning to write a short story and learn to make bread. As well as make the girls' soccer team. I have goals. I just don't go around shouting them out from the housetops, that's all.

Al never does things by halves. This morning, when we started out, she went to the bank to cash her birthday check from her mother. She put half in her savings account. The other half, she informed me, was to be distributed to the poor.

"That's nice," I said.

"If I'm going to be able to live with myself," Al said, "I'm going to share what I have with others. I have to become a better person. I have to grow, to contribute to society."

So what's Joan of Arc got to do with it? I thought, but did not say.

As if I *had* said it, Al said, "Joan of Arc makes us look like a couple of twits, a couple of do-nothings. I mean, there she was, offering herself up to God and country, offering her life and all, when she was a mere girl. It makes you stop and think."

We stomped west on Eighty-sixth Street, thinking glumly about Joan of Arc. Then I spied Polly standing on the far corner, waiting for the light to change. I waved. Polly waved back and stepped out into the traffic. A taxi almost

94

nailed her. I drew in my breath sharply. The driver shouted and shook his fist at Polly.

"You have some kind of death wish, kid?" I said when Polly finally made it across safely.

"My mind was elsewhere," Polly said jauntily. Polly is frequently jaunty. She had on a plaid shirt and shorts and yellow running shoes. "What'll we do to celebrate our last day of freedom?" Polly asked.

"How about the South Street Seaport for laughs?" Al said.

"Or the Museum of Modern Art?" I said. That's long for MOMA.

"We could always hang out on Forty-seventh Street," Al said. That's the heart of the diamond district. Sometimes burglars perpetrate crimes there: break through walls, cut alarm systems, steal gems. Take off with a bag of swag, or loot. Al wants to be there just once, to foil an escape, she says. She plans to tackle the thief and sit on him until the police arrive. Then she plans on taking the perfect diamond she gets as a reward for her heroic act and having it set in her left nostril.

We've spent some time loitering on Forty-seventh Street. The last time we hung around so long, a couple of cops told us to move along.

Al was thrilled. "I bet they think we're going to pull a B and E," she told me. She watches a lot of cop shows. Not me. I like either Ginger Rogers and Fred Astaire or Luciano Pavarotti at the Met. He kills me, that Luciano Pavarotti. He's so cute.

"How about renting a horse to go riding in Central Park?" Polly suggested.

"You're talking big bucks," Al said, scowling. "Very big bucks."

"It costs twenty-two dollars an hour, but if all three of us rode the same horse," Polly said, "it'd be only a little more than seven dollars each."

"Seven dollars would buy quite a lot of food," Al told Polly in a stern tone. Polly blushed and looked at me. I just shrugged.

"Besides," I joked, "if all three of us got on the horse at once, he'd break down, probably. Those Central Park horses are not in their prime."

"I'm the only fat one," Al said. "You two are skinny. It might work, but it costs too much, anyway."

I began to get mad. "Don't be such a killjoy," I told Al. "Everything we say, you put the kibosh on. It's not fair. I thought we were going to have a good time." And I did *not* say "You're not fat," as I've done so often. If Al wants to think she's fat, let her.

Polly laughed nervously. Polly doesn't like Al and me to argue. "I think your grandfather's very handsome," she said, changing the subject. "I told my mother he's more like an actor than a grandfather. He's a regular *bon vivant,* a *boulevardier.* My mother said he sounded like a good extra man to have around for dinner parties." Polly's parents do a lot of entertaining, her father being in the diplomatic service and all.

I looked over at Al, expecting she'd tell Polly about my

grandfather asking her mother out. But I knew by the set of her chin, even by the tip of her ear turned to me, which looked unnaturally pink, that she wasn't going to mention it; she wasn't going to say a word.

Al didn't like the fact that my grandfather had put the moves on her mother. Even if he only asked her to go to the ballet. She was unhappy about it. Probably because my grandfather was old enough, as she said, to be her mother's father.

Tough for her.

In the end, we didn't do much of anything. When there are three of you and only two are enjoying themselves, the third sour one puts a damper on having a good time. That last-day celebration didn't work.

When Polly left us to take a bus back to the west side, Al and I walked home. We didn't say much. I wasn't going to ask her what was bugging her. I was tired of asking her that.

Al may be fourteen, I thought, but she's got a lot of growing up to do.

If I'd known she was going to get bent out of shape that easily, I wouldn't have given her a birthday party at all. Let her go to Burger King. What do I care?

chapter 17

Al smelled. Even in the open air I could smell her.

"What's that perfume you rolled in?" I said.

"I didn't roll in it. All I did was put a drop behind each ear. Isn't it cool? It's Night Song. Stan brought my mother a bottle from Paris."

"Big deal."

"Stan also brought my mother a silk scarf."

"Bigger deal."

I felt Al looking at me. She didn't know what to make of me. Let her figure it out. She better pull up her socks.

"You acted like a twerp yesterday, you know that?"

"I did not." Al's face got red.

"You did, too. And what happened about changing your name? I thought you were going to the minute you got to be fourteen. I thought you were going to make an announcement at the party. You chickened out." I wanted to make her mad. I knew that would get her. I wanted to get even with her for ruining yesterday.

She didn't answer, only speeded up, walking stiff-legged. She was burned up. Good. I let her go. Didn't even run to catch up, the way I usually do. I can manage by myself.

When I got to school, Martha Moseley and her vassals were ensconced by the steps, talking about what glamorous lives they'd led over the summer.

"My father pierced them himself," Martha said, turning this way and that, showing off her pierced ears, her new earrings. "He's a jeweler, you know, and he knows just how to do it so it doesn't hurt. And you have to have real gold earrings so the hole doesn't get infected. Fourteen karat is best."

If Al was here, she'd say something wicked to put Martha in her place. One minute I wanted Al to go, the next I wanted her to be here. Let's face it: I'm still the straight man, she's the silver-tongued orator. I didn't see Linda Benton or Sally Sykes, Martha's chief vassals. Or they had been when school let out in June. There were three new ones. Martha thrived on new vassals. Martha was very demanding, vassalwise. The new ones had smooth, bland faces, anxious-to-please faces. Not faces anyone would willingly choose. Martha preferred ciphers. I bet when and if Martha gets married, she'll choose the three most nothing types she knows to be bridesmaids.

"Where's your old pal Al?" Martha sneered. Al told me Martha practiced sneering every day after school. Even before she ate her yogurt.

I shrugged. "Where's Linda and Sally? You must be lost without them." Martha smiled pityingly. "Sally's moved to Chicago, and Linda's gone to boarding school. She hates it. She says she might run away. It's coed; they have piles of parties after lights out, though. I'm going to visit her next month. I'm flying to Boston and taking the train from there. It'll be quite a trip."

"Why not go by horseback?" I said. "You know, like Paul Revere. 'One if by land, two if by sea.' Right?"

It wasn't great, but it wasn't bad. I galloped up the steps as they tittered behind me. Girls like Martha always titter. And wear fourteen-karat-gold earrings in their pierced ears.

My new home-room teacher was Ms. Bolton. She looked pretty cool. She was long and thin, with long, thin hands and long, thin feet. She wore red tights and kept pushing her hair back nervously. I felt sort of sorry for her. It must be tough being new and tackling a group of eighth-graders.

There were still ten minutes before the opening bell. I went to Mr. Keogh's room to say hello. He was our home-room teacher last year and Al's and my friend. He was the only teacher in the whole school who called Al Al. The others all called her Alexandra.

Al was already there. "So I signed up for shop," I heard her say. "I was the first on the list. I might make a table."

Last year when Al wanted to take shop instead of cooking, they told her she couldn't. Mr. Keogh went to bat for Al. This year girls can take shop and boys can take cooking, if they want. Quite a few do want.

"Hello, there." Mr. Keogh stood up to shake hands with me. "I was wondering where you were. When Al showed up without you, I thought you might be sick. I don't think I've ever seen you apart before." Al and I avoided looking at each other.

"I was fourteen last week," Al told Mr. Keogh. "She," and she lifted her shoulder in my direction, "and her parents gave me a wonderful party to celebrate. It was the most perfect party I ever had."

Kids milled around Mr. Keogh's desk. We only had a couple of minutes before the bell rang.

"One thing, Al, and then you girls had better take off; maybe you better start something small. In shop, I mean," Mr. Keogh said. "A table might be too much at first. Why not start small so you don't get discouraged?"

"Mr. Keogh," Al said, "my name's not Al, anymore."

"It's not? What is it, then?"

Al was silent. "She hasn't made up her mind." I spoke for her. "Maybe Sandy. Maybe Alex. One of those."

"Hello! Mr. Keogh!" Martha Moseley spoke in exclamation points. She twirled and said, "Look at my pierced ears! My father's a jeweler, you know, and he pierced them for me. See my earrings?"

"Well. They're very nice, Martha." Mr. Keogh tugged at his ear. The bell rang then, and he looked very relieved.

Al placed her hands in front of her, and in her deep, dark voice, she said, "Mother Zandi says she who pierces ears has hole in head."

That broke Mr. Keogh up. He laughed so hard the new kids in his class looked at each other, as if to say, "This guy's a nut case."

"Go along, girls. I'll talk to you later," he said.

"I'm sorry," Al said when we were halfway down the hall.

"Me, too," I told her.

Martha Moseley huffed her way past us, her behind wiggling in indignation.

That made things just about perfect.

chapter 18

"The trouble with me is," Al confessed, "I'm always standing back and looking at myself, contemplating my own navel. I'm too uptight. I know that. I wish I was more of a free spirit. I want to be a free spirit, but I can't seem to cut it."

"You're a nonconformist," I told her, "and that's a good way to be. You're tense because you're afraid you might be too much of a nonconformist, that's all."

Al stared at me. "You think that's it?"

"Sure. Smile more. People like people who smile."

Al put a finger in each corner of her mouth and pulled her mouth as wide as it could go.

"How's that?" she said.

I told her, "Not bad."

"As I grow older," Al went on, "I'm becoming less of a nonconformist than when I was thirteen. That's one thing being fourteen has done to me. It's made me cautious. Sort of apprehensive, if you know what I mean. But darned if I'm going to be totally conformist. Ever."

"I don't think there's much danger of that," I said.

"Conformists are boring," Al said. "I may be a pain in the neck, but I'm never going to be a *boring* pain in the neck."

We got a good laugh out of that.

"You know who's uptight? Ms. Bolton."

Al pulled my arm, warning me. "Shhh, there she is."

Ms. Bolton came out of the teachers' room right ahead of us. Her head was down. I don't think she knew we were there. She had on her red tights. We figured she must have about ten pairs of red tights.

As if she'd heard us, Ms. Bolton turned, saw us, and said, "Hello, kids." Probably she hadn't memorized our names yet. We said hello back. I think she's shy. Al says she's aloof. Whatever. Yesterday we peeked into the teachers' room and saw Ms. Bolton sitting by herself, mournfully eating a sandwich. The other teachers give her a lot of room.

We slowed down and followed her slowly. By the time we reached the street, Ms. Bolton was gone.

"Mr. Keogh seems down in the dumps," Al told me. "He wasn't his usual friendly self today."

"Maybe his marriage is in trouble."

"No, he told me he had to put his father in an old people's home just before school started," Al said. "He said it almost broke his heart. He goes to see his father every weekend, sometimes twice. His father has a wonky heart and hardening of the arteries. He didn't want to go into the home. He'd been in the same apartment for almost forty years, Mr. Keogh said. Then his father fell and couldn't get up. Mr. Keogh's mother died four years ago, so he's all alone. So they had to put him in the home.

"You know something? Kids think they have problems. But we're pretty sure things will fall into place when we grow up and go into the world. We think the only reason we have problems is that we're young. So then you look around and you see people like Ms. Bolton, who's probably unhappy and lonely, and Mr. Keogh's father, who's old and unhappy because he doesn't want to be in the home, and Mr. Keogh, who's unhappy because his father's unhappy. So what good does it do to grow up? It doesn't solve anything.

"What it all boils down to, my friend," Al gave me the owl eye, "is that happiness is elusive. The more you look for it, the more elusive it becomes."

"Maybe the trick is not to look for it," I said, "and maybe it'll creep up on you when you least expect it."

"You want to come with me? I'm going to the card shop to buy a card to send to Brian."

"What kind of card?"

"One of those 'Oooops, sorry I forgot' cards."

"What'd you forget?"

"His birthday. He sent me an 'Oooops, sorry I forgot' card after Louise told him I'd had a big birthday party."

"How come you didn't tell me?"

"It was when we were mad at each other. I wanted to tell you, but I was too mad at you. Anyway, it turns out," Al flashed me a big grin, "his birthday was two days before mine. How do you like them apples? He's sixteen. Two years and two days older'n me."

"Well, I guess that means you're opening up a whole new phase in your relationship," I said. "Go for it, kid."

"Does bad luck seem to follow you?" Al said in her swami voice. "Has the one you love found another? I, Mother Zandi, will set you on the right path, warn you gravely, suggest wisely, explain fully."

"Bag it, Mother Zandi," I said.

chapter 19

"Grandfather's asked Al's mother out on a date," I said, watching my mother closely, thinking, hoping actually, she'd freak when she heard the news.

"I know," she said calmly. "He told me. Isn't that nice? I'm sure they'll enjoy each other's company."

"He's pretty old for her, don't you think?" I said, in a severe way designed to intimidate her. "I mean, when you think about it, he's old enough to be her father."

"So he is. If he's old enough to be my father," my mother said, "he's old enough to be Al's mother's father. However, I do believe she's several years older than I am." My mother sat up straight and stretched out her neck in an effort to eliminate unwanted bulges.

"Al says she's forty-four or forty-five," I said. "She doesn't remember exactly what year she was born."

"Ah, yes." My mother smiled. "The old failing memory trick. I know it well. They'll have a fine time. Cool your jets," my mother told me. I hate it when she talks like that, as if she were my age. It's very undignified, I think.

"Grandfather's taking Al's mother to the ballet," I told my father. Maybe *he'd* jump up and down and say, "I won't have it!"

"Is that so?" He looked over the top of his newspaper at me. "I didn't know they knew each other."

"Dad," I said very patiently, "they met here, in this apartment. At Al's party."

"Oh, so they did, so they did." My father disappeared behind his paper. I directed a couple of laser beam stares at him, thinking how cool it would be if the paper went up in smoke before his very eyes.

But nothing happened, as it so often does.

The big question I ask myself often is: is my father as out of it as he pretends to be, or is it a ruse he uses when he doesn't want to get involved? Men, fathers particularly, can be pretty sneaky at times, I've discovered.

As luck would have it, Teddy was lurking. Scratching himself and lurking. Teddy's fading fast. His spots now look like freckles on their way out. He's full of pent-up energy. He's going back to school on Monday. The whole family is offering up thanks for small favors.

"I heard you!" Teddy screeched. "I heard you! Don't think you can keep it a secret from me! Al's mother's going out with our grandfather. What's going on here, anyway?" Teddy scrooched up his face into a tight knot. I couldn't get over his resemblance to my favorite baby monkey at the zoo.

"Keep your hair on, kid," I told Teddy. "It's strictly a platonic friendship."

Teddy clapped his hands over his mouth. His beady little eyes sparkled gleefully.

"I'm telling, I'm telling!" he crooned from behind his hands. "A platonic friendship, huh?" Teddy was onto some pretty hot stuff here. He went happily into the bathroom, complete with fins and mask. Teddy liked nothing better than to go snorkeling in the tub. Usually he sings while preparing himself for descent.

"My bonnie lies over the ocean," I heard Teddy shouting. "My bonnie lies over the sea."

Someone had told Teddy that the song was very dirty. My mother said it was dirty only if you had a dirty mind.

Teddy was crestfallen when she said that. Which was a joy in itself. Nothing I like better than to see that kid's crest fall.

If I want to make his day, I bang on the bathroom door while he's singing and cry, "The sheriff's on his way to arrest you if you don't quit singing that dirty song!" So, feeling big-hearted, I did just that.

I banged and shouted, and I could hear Teddy gurgling with pleasure as he submerged.

I mean, you can hear dirtier songs in your friendly neighborhood record shop. Any day of the week.

chapter 20

Saturday was hot and muggy. Thick clouds scudded overhead. Planes coming into LaGuardia and Kennedy flew low, parting the clouds as if they were nothing.

"I love flying through clouds," Al said. "You feel as if you're nowhere—you're suspended above the earth and you're not sure if you're coming down or going up."

Al's flown a lot. I never have. Everyone I know flies. Even Melvin Ticknor went to Cancún last summer. His mother got divorced and she heard there were lots of single guys down there, plus she owed herself a trip. She took Melvin along to Mexico. He got Montezuma's revenge and never got out of the motel room. Melvin's mother wants to go back next year, to see if this golf pro she met is still there. Melvin says he wouldn't be caught dead there. "Didn't see nothing but the bathroom," Melvin told me glumly. "That and lousy TV."

Al looked up as a 747 flew so low it practically ruffled our hair. "What if one of those bozos crashed?" she asked me.

"Chaos," I told her, not wanting to dwell on it. I thought I saw tiny heads at the plane's windows, but I couldn't be sure.

We waited on the corner where we'd seen the woman with the eyes. We must've waited half an hour. Al had a five dollar bill to give her. The digital clock said it was 77 degrees, and 11:07. The woman didn't show. "Maybe the police told her to move along," Al said.

I said, "Maybe she's dead."

"Now who's putting a damper on the fun?" Al said.

When at last we gave up and walked west, we were in search of Rudy. It seemed like a good time to listen to some of his fantastic tales. He always cheered us up. We checked all his familiar haunts. He wasn't around. Finally, we went up to a guy playing a mournful guitar on the corner of Forty-fifth Street.

"Do you know Rudy?" Al said.

The guy scratched his carefully arranged black hair. "What's he play?"

"Violin."

"Oh, that Rudy. Gotcha." His wide black mustache rippled as he talked. "He's took off, I hear from the grapevine."

"Took off? Where to?" Al and I said, practically in unison. "He wouldn't leave without telling us good-bye," I said.

"Yeah, well, the way I heard it," the guy put on his cowboy hat and smiled at a passing pretty girl, "Rudy came on hard times. Somebody stole his violin. He went looking in every pawnshop on the west side, not to mention the east side. Never found it. I hear he was pretty down, pretty discouraged. He went to Florida. St. Pete, around there. His brother lives down there. Maybe it's his sister. I don't know. He said he'd never find another violin like that one. He was pretty broke up, I heard. It was his father's violin, very valuable, they say. Came from Germany. Or maybe Austria." The man's eyebrows went up. "What do I know?"

"Rudy was from Brooklyn," I said. "Coney Island."

"All I know is what I'm telling you." Two more pretty girls stopped to buy a pretzel from a street vendor and the guy began to serenade them with a spirited tune, flashing his eyes, taking tiny steps, inviting them to dance with him. They turned their backs and walked away, not giving him a second glance.

"Sorry, girls," the guitar player called in a loud voice as we walked away. We looked back, not knowing if he was talking to us or to the girls who'd ignored him.

"Rudy wouldn't have taken off like that, without letting us know," Al said.

"How could he let us know? He didn't even know our last names," I said. "Or where we live. He didn't know

112

anything about us. When you come right down to it, he didn't know squat about us. We knew about him, or what he told us about himself. We'll probably never see him again."

"We'll never find that woman, either. I feel it in my bones." Al's shoulders slumped, and she fumbled in her pocket for the five dollars. We both looked at the money stupidly, as if wondering how it had gotten there.

"The city's too big," I told her. "You hardly ever find anyone you're looking for."

"Let's go to St. Patrick's," Al said. "Sit down and smell the incense." Al was crazy about the smell of incense.

"All right," I said. St. Patrick's Cathedral is beautiful and vast. It makes me feel as if I'm in Europe when I go there. There are lots of cathedrals in Europe, I understand. St. Patrick's may be as close as I'll ever get to Europe.

We sat and watched the people taking pictures, wandering around, admiring everything. On our way out, there was a box marked For the Poor of the World. Al carefully folded her money and slipped it in the slot. We went down the church steps, and the humidity made us gasp.

"At least I did something positive," Al told me.

"That beats nothing," I said.

chapter 21

"How's your little boy?" I asked Mr. Keogh when Al and I stopped to see him Monday morning on our way to class.

"He's a pistol. Turned two last week. We gave him a set of blocks for his birthday. First thing he did was make a towering structure which he says is a church. My wife thinks he's aiming to be an architect. I think he might be aiming to be a priest." Mr. Keogh grinned. "Hard to tell, at this age."

Mr. Keogh fiddled with a pencil.

"I have a favor to ask of you," he said.

"So ask," Al said.

"Right. Well, here it is." Mr. Keogh cleared his throat.

"If you're not busy next Saturday morning, how about coming with me to visit my father in his nursing home?"

I looked at Al, and she looked back. Flabbergast city.

"To do what?" Al got out.

"Talk. Read to them, the old people, I mean. Sing songs, if you want." Mr. Keogh tapped his teeth with the pencil. "The point is, they need distraction. Most of them sit in the same chairs, in the same places, day after day. They watch television, but that's about it. Lethargy sets in and it's bad for them. They lose interest in things, in life. The doctors asked me, after they found out I was a teacher, if I knew any kids who might be willing to visit the patients. They've experimented and found that old people benefit greatly from contact with young people. Just having them around, the doctors said, is extremely beneficial, even for a short while.

"So I thought of you right off. You're good kids. I wouldn't ask just anyone to come up there with me." Mr. Keogh smiled tentatively at us.

Al said, "I could tell their fortunes."

"Great! Who doesn't like to have their fortunes told?"

"I can't do anything," I told Mr. Keogh. "I can play the harmonica but only a little." I wasn't at all sure I wanted to spend Saturday morning talking to a bunch of old fogies.

"Harmonica's great, too. Fortunes are always good." I had the feeling if one of us said we could pick pockets, Mr. Keogh would say, "Great! Picking pockets is always good for a laugh."

"It's purely an experiment, don't forget," Mr. Keogh said. Then the bell rang and we breathed a sigh of relief. It had been a short but stressful interview. We said all right, we'd go. Mr. Keogh said he'd pick us up Saturday morning outside our apartment at ten sharp.

"Thanks, girls." He shook hands. "You won't regret this, I promise you. You're doing a good deed, and maybe both of you will benefit from it, just as my father and the rest of them will benefit from having you there."

"I'm not hot on this deal," I said, as Al and I hurried back to our home room. "I don't know what to say to them."

"Neither do I. But I'll say this." Al's eyes glittered. "This is our chance to make something of ourselves, to do something selfless. We're getting points in heaven for this one, baby."

"I'm not out to get points in heaven," I told her.

"I don't know why not." Al's eyebrows did their disappearing act. "You need all the points you can get."

How does she know I need points?

She has some nerve.

When I told my mother about Al and me going to the old people's home to cheer them up, she flipped. I mean, you would've thought I'd said I was going to become Florence Nightingale.

"Marvelous!" she exclaimed, giving me a bear hug and an approving look. She frequently gives me bear hugs. Approving looks are in shorter supply. While I basked in my mother's approval, a dismaying thought crept into my head.

Suppose they're deaf? Lots of old people were, I knew. Suppose they couldn't hear when I played my harmonica? Well, I was so bad at it, it might be a good thing if they were deaf. Still, knocking myself out on the harmonica for a bunch of deaf oldsters has got to be straight out of a Fellini movie. Fellini is an Italian movie director who deals in the existential absurdities of life.

Maybe Martha Moseley could come with us and give a lecture on pierced ears and fourteen-karat-gold earrings. That oughta get her points in heaven, too. Which, I figure, she needs a heck of a lot more than I do.

When I went down the hall to Al's to discuss our plans for the oldsters, she was deep in her math homework. If Fellini had ever observed Al doing her math homework, he would've signed her to a ten-year contract on the spot. Math is Al's worst subject. She sweats bullets over it.

"I'll come back when you're done," I said.

"No! Stay. I'm almost finished." I read a fashion magazine and listened to her breathing. When I heard her slam her book closed, I knew she was through.

"I wish I hadn't said I'd go," I said. "I won't know what to say, what to do. I don't know anything about how to treat old people."

Al looked surprised. "How about your grandfather?" she asked.

"He's not old old, he's just old," I said.

"No offense, but to some people he might be considered

old old." Al hadn't brought up the subject of her mother and my grandfather's date again. Neither had I.

"I guess we just play it by ear," I said. "Just act natural."

"Listen." Al held up a finger and waved it under my nose. "I read the Diary of Anne Frank last night."

"Again?" We've read that diary about a hundred times, each of us.

"She was only our age when she said, 'I felt lonely, but hardly ever in despair!' That's when she was shut up in that room, hiding from the Nazis. How do you like that? She said she'd hardly ever been in despair. It makes me ashamed of myself when I read that. Doesn't it make you ashamed?"

"No," I said. "She wrote that diary to keep herself sane. I'm sure of that. If it hadn't been for those creeps that gave her away, the Nazis never would've found her hiding place."

"The world is full of creeps," Al told me. "I know I agitate too much about trivial things. Like, am I popular, am I pretty, am I a winner? And we all know the answers to those, right?" Al began to pace. "But I'll tell you one thing. I can't help it. I think about those things. Am I an achiever? Heck, no. But I'm smart." She turned to look at me, and I saw tears in her eyes. Reading Anne Frank did that to us, me and her. "Chalk one up, for me. Am I gorgeous? Heck, no. But I might be someday. Am I a winner? Heck, no, but someday my name may be a household word."

"What's the household word?" I asked because I knew she wanted me to.

"Try Comet," she said. "Or how about Listerine?"

"Would you settle for Pepperidge Farm?"

"I have often been in the pits," Al said, "but never forever. Do you ever wonder what you'd do if you were in Anne Frank's shoes?"

As long as I've known Al, I've never gotten used to the way she switches subjects.

"That's like saying do you know what you'd do if somebody pulled a knife on you," I said. "You can't know until you're actually faced with something terrible."

"It just so happened that Anne Frank and Joan of Arc had the strength and the inner fortitude to face death without flinching." Al stood in front of the mirror, looking at herself.

"Is that the face of someone with inner fortitude?" she asked her face. Then she answered, "Heck, no, it's the face of an abject coward."

Then, switching to her swami voice, Al said, "Mother Zandi detects the odor of dead fish. The fish stinks from its head. Evil is everywhere. 'To thine own self be true' and bad luck will take a different road. The one you love will love you back."

"You're full of it, Mother Zandi," I said.

"We'll wow those senior citizens, kid," Al told me. "I know we will."

chapter 22

Mr. Keogh's beat-up station wagon was almost full when he picked us up promptly at ten Saturday morning. Two seventh-grade twerps were in back and two girls about our age from Mr. Keogh's neighborhood were in front. Al and I climbed in the middle. Mr. Keogh introduced us. Nobody spoke as we rattled our way up to the Bronx. I looked over at Al. She was staring out the window and biting her nails. Let me out of here, I thought.

What if they were handicapped? Or had goiters, those things old people got that looked as if they had rubber tires around their necks. Maybe they were losing their marbles, or didn't know what year it was or what their names were. I didn't know if I could cope.

The home was U-shaped and painted a pale, sickly green, with aluminum awnings and dusty geraniums lining the path to the front door. Above the door a sign said Sunlight Manor. Across the street a used car lot advertised Super Buys! and Cream Puffs for Sale.

Maybe it wasn't a used car lot, I thought; maybe it was a bakery disguised as a used car lot.

An attendant in a white coat met us and said, "They're waiting for you," in what seemed to me an ominous tone. Mr. Keogh led the way up a flight of stairs.

"Don't forget, kids," he said nervously, "we're all feeling our way here. I'm new at this, too. Remember: if it's worth doing at all, it's worth doing well. Hold the thought."

He stopped outside a door at the top of the stairs. "Well, here we are," he said. The door opened, and a tall man with steel gray hair came out and shook Mr. Keogh's hand.

"I'm Dr. Simon," the man said. "We're so glad you could come. We're all looking forward to this very much. Please come in."

Mr. Keogh led the way. We almost clung to his coattails in an effort to stay close to him.

"Do any of you know how to play the piano?" Dr. Simon asked. "Music is always a good icebreaker."

There seemed to be a lot of old people in the room. Nobody looked at us or indicated any interest in us. They all looked very clean and very old. My grandfather would look like a teenager in this crowd, I thought. I looked at

Al to see what she was thinking. Her face was totally without expression.

"Donny does," Mr. Keogh said, indicating one of the seventh-grade boys. Donny went to the grand piano in a corner of the room, sat down, and punched on the keys until they gave up a tune, which I finally figured out after a couple minutes was "God Bless America." Donny performed with great aplomb, as if he was Leonard Bernstein. His mother would've been proud. His music teacher, if he had one, ought to be shot.

Donny kept punching away, and music filled the hall. A tall, stout lady in a black dress with pearls and a veil over her blue hair got up, went to the piano and rested one hand lightly on it, and sang. She knew a lot of the words, and those she didn't know she faked. Some of the others joined in, their reedy voices rising and falling. The woman in black got with it and wound up belting out the words like she was Kate Smith at the opening game of the World Series. When she and Donny were through, she bowed to the left, then to the right, eliciting a smattering of applause.

I felt as if I had about a dozen arms and legs and none of them was the right size. It was like being at a boy-girl party and not knowing where to sit, where to look, how to act, whom to talk to.

Then I heard a sound like escaping steam.

"Ssssstt," it said. "Ssssstt." I followed the sound with my eyes, which lit on a tiny plump little woman in a cardigan sweater sitting on a couch all by herself.

"Sit down," she said. "In my day I could've sung rings

around her. But my day is past, and I'm smart enough to know it. Unlike lots of people I could mention." She wore diamond rings on both her tiny spotted hands, which moved constantly, emphasizing her words.

"Here." She handed me a weekly magazine. "Read this. I forgot my eyeglasses. I don't need them. My eyes are perfectly good. Glasses are so disfiguring, don't you think? Start at the beginning, and I'll tell you when to stop."

No please, no nothing.

The magazine was open to the Personals. Personals are so bizarre. I love to read them.

I began at the first Personal.

"Successful, handsome, slim business exec wants female counterpart to share good times, music, laughter, dancing in white tie or jeans." Then there was a box number to reply to, care of the magazine.

The little woman nodded vigorously, obviously pleased. "They all want 'em handsome and successful and slim," she said, very knowing. "I wonder what'd happen if somebody fat and unsuccessful and ugly put in an ad. There must be a lot of fat, unsuccessful, ugly people out there who want love and good times. But then, nobody really sees themself, do they? Go on."

I did as I was told.

"I am bright, beautiful, great figure," the ad read. The woman cackled delightedly. "Sure, sure, I know all about your great figure!" she cried. "Keep going, keep going!" she told me.

I felt like saying, "Stop interrupting me," but did not.

"Outgoing, sensitive, elegant," I read. "Seek exceptional unmarried male with high standards, possible long-term relationship."

"High standards! High standards!" the tiny woman shouted. "What do they know about high standards! Advertising in a magazine, telling all the world how beautiful they are, how great their figure is. Blowing their own horn. It's a good thing my mother isn't alive. Such goings on." The woman put her hand on my arm, pinching it ever so slightly. Her eyes sparkled with malice. "Advertising in a magazine for a husband. Or, better yet, a lover. Scandalous!"

The older I get, the weirder people are. This one was a dilly. I read the whole page of Personals to the tiny woman. Then she fell into a doze. One minute her eyes were snapping, the next she was asleep. I left her and went to find Al.

She was surrounded by a circle of old folks.

"Mother Zandi says," I heard her say. She was giving them the swami bit. "Lovers may demand more of your time than you can give," she said in her deep, dark voice. "Look for a surprise in your mailbox. The jet-set routine may get boring this week. Take it easy, have some friends in for cards. Shoot it up."

They loved it. That last about shooting it up brought down the house. One man laughed so hard he started to choke and had to be slapped on the back until he got his breath.

Al was having a blast. I could tell from her face. I don't

think she ever tried her Mother Zandi routine on anyone before. Before me, that is. It and she were a hit.

Donny and the other boy played chopsticks on the piano until Mr. Keogh had to tell them to stop. I saw the two girls from Mr. Keogh's neighborhood. It looked as if they were being given knitting lessons by a couple of old ladies who had long, half-knitted mufflers growing out of their laps. The girls were paying close attention as the mufflers got longer and longer. They'd be great for a couple of giraffes, I figured.

I saw Mr. Keogh and an old man playing chess. That must be Mr. Keogh's father, I thought. There was a resemblance.

Somebody played some records. Two women danced together, the smaller one leading her partner in a series of intricate steps. I hoped maybe there'd be refreshments soon.

Suddenly Al was there, grabbing my arm until it hurt.

"Did you see him?"

"Who? No."

"There." She pointed.

Standing by the record player, his back to us, was a small man.

"So? What's the big deal?" I said.

"Wait." I felt Al's breath on my cheek. She was pale, and her eyes almost popped out of her head, she was so excited.

The small man turned. It was Mr. Richards. "Oh, no," I sighed. "No, it's not him."

"See? I'm not imagining it." Al stepped back to look at me. "You thought I was dreaming, didn't you? Or hallucinating."

"What'll we do?" I kept looking at him. This man was older than Mr. Richards. His face was very lined, and he had a slight hump on his back.

"It's not really him," I told Al. "He just looks a lot like him."

"That's *your* story." Al narrowed her eyes at me. "Let's talk to him. That way we'll be sure."

"You go," I told her. "I'll wait here."

"Oh, no, you don't. This is something we do together," Al said.

She was right. I knew she was right, but I was scared.

"When we hear his voice," Al said, nudging me toward the man, "then we'll know for sure."

"I don't remember how Mr. Richards sounded," I said. "I remember everything about him except the sound of his voice."

"Close your eyes," Al commanded. "OK. Now can't you hear him hollering, 'Glide, glide,' the way he did when we were trying to skate on his kitchen floor?"

I closed my eyes and tried. I really did.

I opened my eyes. "Come on." Al grabbed me, forcing me to walk with her to where the little man stood.

"I know who you are," the little man said to me. "And you must be Alexandra."

I swallowed hard. Al wouldn't let go of my arm.

"Everybody calls me Al," she said in a weak voice.

"How did you know our names?" I got out.

"Oh, I have ways." His eyes, as blue as Mr. Richards's, twinkled. "I get around." That definitely was not Mr. Richards's voice.

"My name's William, but everybody calls me Billy," he said.

"No offense," Al said, "but are you a retired bartender?"

"No such luck," Billy said. "Insurance salesman. Long term. Why, I could write a policy so fast your eyes'd smart."

I had to see his arm. Mr. Richards had Home Sweet Home tattooed on his right arm. I had to see.

"Could I please see your right arm?" I said timidly. Sometimes the direct approach is best. I heard Al gasp.

"Well, now." He pulled up the sleeve of his sweater, unbuttoned his cuff, and thrust a bare arm at us. No tattoo.

"You want to see the other arm?" Al nodded, and he did the same with the other sleeve. Still no tattoo.

"Thank you," I mumbled.

"Don't mention it."

"We had a very good friend who died," I explained. "You look just like him. We thought it was him for a minute."

"I'm sorry," he said.

"It's time for us to go," Mr. Keogh said, car keys dangling from his hand.

Dr. Simon saw us to the door.

"Thank you for coming," he said. "I know they enjoyed having you. Perhaps you'll come again?"

"John," Mr. Keogh's father tugged at his jacket, "tell your mother I won't be home for dinner tonight, please. I have business commitments I must attend to."

Mr. Keogh put his arm around his father. "Yes, Dad, I'll tell her," he said.

The plump little woman I'd read the Personals to said, "He's a penny pincher," and she jabbed her finger at a man standing beside her. "He squeezes a nickel so hard it shouts."

"And you, my dear," said the man, without rancor, "are a gold digger."

We went back to the station wagon, and Mr. Keogh drove off. He let me and Al off first.

"I think it went very well," he told us. "Thanks for a good job well done. I knew I could count on you."

"You want to come in for lunch?" I asked Al as we went up in the elevator.

She shook her head. "No, thanks. I've got piles of stuff to do. I was glad we went, though. Weren't you? I mean, I actually *did* something for somebody. Without thinking of myself. We were being selfless." Al congratulated herself. And me.

"Not entirely," I said. "We didn't want to go, but we did. OK. Big step forward. But after we got there, it wasn't all that bad. It was sort of fun. I watched you being Mother Zandi. You loved it. I got a kick out of reading the Personals to that old lady.

"What if somebody said, 'Today you have to work in a shelter for the homeless? You've got to sleep there, listen to the sounds, eat the food. Use the toilets. Smell the smells.' "

"Talk about being a killjoy," Al said, scowling at me. "You're an ace."

"Maybe. But that would be another ball of wax, wouldn't it?"

"Who's going to ask somebody our age to do something like that? And what would we accomplish by doing it?"

"I don't know. I'm just saying what if? That's all."

Al thought about what I'd said. I could almost hear her thinking.

"I don't think I know *how* to be totally selfless," she said at last, sadly. "It's hard to put yourself in someone else's place."

"Yeah. I know."

Al fumbled for her key. *"Adiós,"* she said.

"See you," I answered. Once inside, I stood in my room and looked at it. It was all mine. I didn't have to share it with anyone.

I don't know how to be selfless, either, I realized. I can learn, I told myself. I will try to learn. That's the best I can do, is try.

chapter 23

Sunday Polly called and asked me over for lunch.

"Bring Al," Polly said.

"It's Sunday. Her togetherness day with her mother," I told Polly. I decided to wait until I got there to tell her about yesterday. I decided, too, to make a good story better. I'd work on it going over on the bus.

Holding a hand mirror, I checked out my profile in the bathroom. Maybe I could use a nose job, too, like Thelma. My nose was nothing to write home about, but it doesn't offend me. It was the rest of me that cried out for plastic surgery. I read about a woman who had a plastic surgeon take a tuck in her fanny. She couldn't sit down for three months. She even had to eat standing up. What some people will do to have a beautiful behind is beyond me.

The bell rang. I opened the door a crack and said, "I gave at the office." Then I got a good look and shrieked. Al had on the black satin turban and the piece of material Polly had given her for her birthday. It was draped around her and left one shoulder bare. Her red shoes peeked out from underneath. She looked about eight feet tall. She had also painted her eyebrows and her mouth and her cheeks, so she looked like something out of Punch and Judy.

"Mother Zandi says can you spare a cup of sugar?" Al said.

"What are you doing here on Sunday?" I opened the door so she could get in. Walking was not easy for her, what with her clunky shoes and the garment she wore.

"Guess what? My mother asked me if I minded if we didn't do something together today. Can you beat it? Naturally I didn't tell her that was cool, that this Sunday togetherness drill can be a drag on occasion."

"Come to Polly's, then. She asked us for lunch. I told her you couldn't make it. Now you can."

"My mother has a date."

"That's nice."

"Don't you want to know who with?"

Oh, oh. Here we go again.

I decided to tough it out. "Who?" I said.

"Stan. They're going to some bigwig fracas at the Plaza. She said she hoped I wouldn't mind." Al made owl eyes at me. "She has a snazzy new dress."

"So Stan's back in the picture." Good. "He's nice, right?"

"He's all right. He's more her age. You know."

"Sure. He's got megabucks, too. That makes him pretty cute."

"Your grandfather's much cuter," Al said.

I didn't say anything. She was bound and determined to talk about my grandfather.

"If your grandfather and my mother had gotten married," Al began.

I whomped myself on the forehead and said, "Oh, no! I don't believe you. You are totally weird."

"Let me finish." As if I could stop her.

"They have one date and you've got them going down the aisle," I said. "You're nuts."

"If your grandfather and my mother had gotten married," Al started all over, "you and I would have been related to each other."

I just shook my head. Al's face got red. "Well, it's true. We would have."

"What would we have been? Stepsisters? Like in Cinderella?" I asked, very sarcastically.

"If they had," Al plowed on, "then *my* mother would've been *your* mother's stepmother. So you see," she finished complacently.

I swallowed twice. Then I said, "You floor me. You put me totally under the rug."

"It's true. Figure it out. If my mother and . . ."

I put up my hand like a traffic cop. "Enough. Go wash your face, clean up your act, and get your buns back here

132

so we can go to Polly's. My mother and Teddy went to Connecticut, and my father's somewhere."

"Every time Teddy goes to Connecticut, he comes back more suave than the time before," Al observed. "This time he'll probably return with an Afro and L. L. Bean hunting boots."

When we finally got going, it was raining. We hopped on the bus. Al took a window seat. She likes to look out.

"Isn't that Ms. Bolton?" she said, wiping off the window with the sleeve of her sweater, which was looped around her neck. Very preppy.

I leaned across to see out. "I think so. They look like her red tights. Who's she with?"

"Some hunk."

I saw them. Ms. Bolton was looking at him and laughing. Her hair was wet and sort of stringy. Her face was happy.

"She looks radiant," Al said. "I've never seen anyone look truly radiant before." The bus stopped at a red light. We watched them go into a restaurant.

"Do you think being in love makes people look radiant?" I said.

"You're asking *me?* Your basic radiant-in-love teenager? You've got the wrong guy."

Al stared out at the rain. "I like the idea that there are two of me," she said.

"I only see one," I replied.

"There's me, just plain Al. Then there's Mother Zandi. I can say and do things when I'm Mother Zandi that I can't say and do as just plain Al. So, in effect, I'm two people."

"A split personality, you mean."

"Well, sort of. And you know something else?"

I let her have her head, as they say about horses.

"I finally figured it out." Al shoved her bangs around. "It doesn't matter what your name is as long as you've got it all together. As long as you're doing the best you can. It's up to you."

"You know, I've been thinking," I said. "My birthday's next week. I'll be thirteen, a real teenager. And guess what?"

"What?"

I smiled at Al. "I'm thinking of changing my name. How about that?"

In answer, Al threw her sweater over my head. She wouldn't take it off. I kicked her in the shins, and we struggled. Then we got laughing so hard we couldn't stop.

"Last stop!" the bus driver hollered. Al finally let me out from under. The driver glared at us. "End of the line," he told us sternly.

"Oh, no, sir," Al said, with great respect. "It's only the beginning. Only the beginning."

"Don't get fresh with me," he said.